PRAISE FOR A BAD GOD'S GUIDE TO BEING GOOD

"This bad boy's journey is a laugh-out-loud delight, packed with cartoons and footnotes, perfect for fans of The Wimpy Kid."
The Daily Mail

"Outrageously funny ... Sharp wit, ethical dilemmas, sly mythological references and oodles of doodles are a recipe for pure reading pleasure."
THE GUARDIAN

"Laugh-out-loud funny, whip-smart observation, totally original & all round EPIC."
Hannah Gold
author of The Last Bear

"Forget Thor, it's Louie who really brings the thunder with this book. Action-packed, smart and very, very funny."
Rob Biddulph
author of Draw With Rob

"OFTEN LAUGH-OUT-LOUD FUNNY, THIS IS AN IRREVERENT ROMP THROUGH PRACTICAL MORAL PHILOSOPHY, LIKE NETFLIX'S THE GOOD PLACE WITH MORE SNARKY CARTOON SNAKES."
The Observer

"A sheer doodle-filled comic delight."
DOMINIQUE VALENTE
author of Starfell

This book belongs to:

LOKI

LOUIE STOWELL

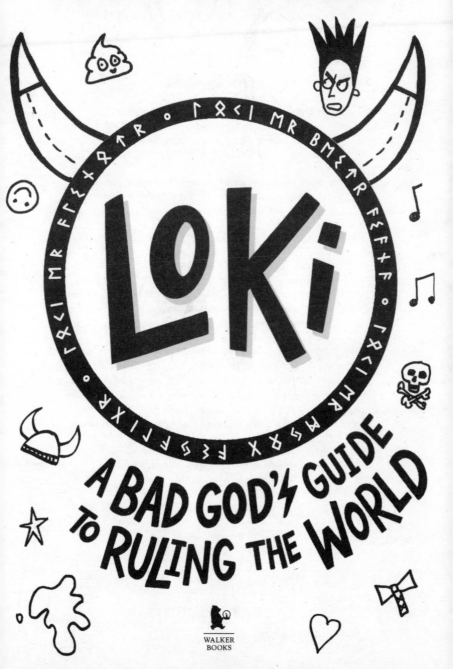

LOKI

A BAD GOD'S GUIDE TO RULING THE WORLD

WALKER
BOOKS

First published 2023 by Walker Books Ltd
87 Vauxhall Walk, London SE11 5HJ

2 4 6 8 10 9 7 5 3 1

This book has been typeset in Autumn Voyage, Avenir,
Bembo, Blackout, Cabazon, ITC American Typewriter,
Liquid Embrace, Neato Serif, Open Sans, Times and WB Loki

Printed and bound by CPI Group (UK) Ltd, Croydon CR0 4YY

British Library Cataloguing in Publication Data:
a catalogue record for this book is available
from the British Library

ISBN 978-1-5295-0123-0

www.walker.co.uk

WALKER
BOOKS

FSC
www.fsc.org
MIX
Paper | Supporting
responsible forestry
FSC® C171272

To Isildur,
for being a warning to us all.

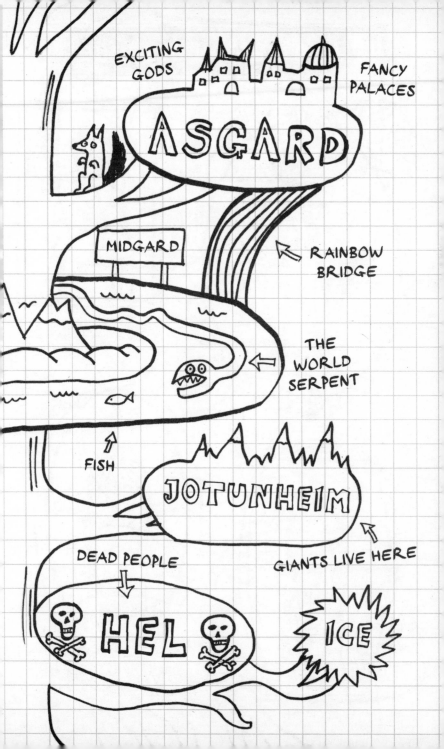

Dramatis Personae

FIDO

HEIMDALL

HYRROKKIN

BALDER

ODIN

FIERCE BOY ONE

Timetable

		Monday	Tuesday
1		MATHS	MATHS
2		ART	HAND-WRITING
3		SPELLING	ENGLISH
4		TOPIC	GEOGRAPHY
5		PE	SCIENCE

LOKI vs LUNCHBREAK

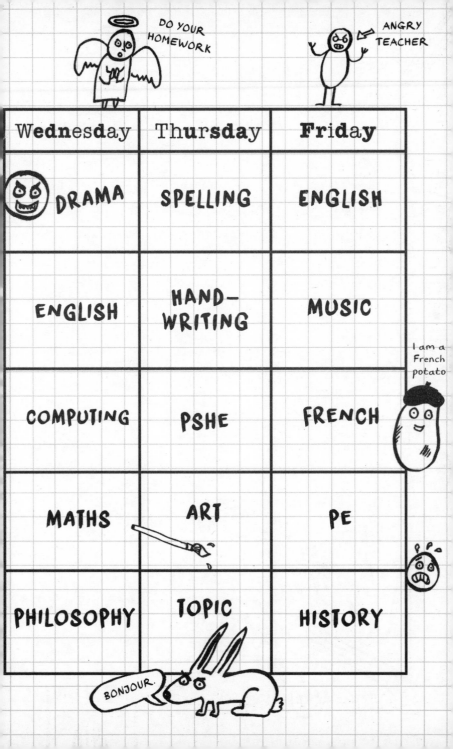

Welcome to this work of genius!

About this book:

This is a magical diary, which should be a wondrous thing but in reality it is a living nightmare. Every time I, Loki, god of mischief, record my deeds inside its pages, the diary calculates my so-called virtue score. This calculation rarely goes in my favour.

And to make matters worse, if I stray ever so slightly from the truth, it corrects me. I have to put up with such nonsense because this diary is programmed with the so-called wisdom of smelly bum bum Odin.

> **Correction: Odin does not have a smelly bum bum.**

!

ODIN'S WISDOM →

HA! Victory! I made the diary say "smelly bum bum"!

Anyway. I have been sent to Midgard, which you peasants call Earth, as punishment for cutting off the goddess Sif's hair. The conditions of my punishment are that I must take the form of a mortal child and refrain from displaying my amazing godly powers. Luckily, I've discovered a loophole: as long as mortals don't SEE me transforming into various animals and beings, I can do it as often as I like.

! This is, irritatingly, true.

Accompanying me are my fake family: Thor, Hyrrokkin and Heimdall.

This is what I have done on Earth so far...

Discovered the horrors of mortal school.

Made two mortal friends.

Valerie Georgina

Defeated many Frost Giants!

Oh no! Oh no!

(Well, the same ones twice.)

Woohoo! Woohoo!

And received magical gifts...

A GIANT'S GUIDE TO MAGIC SPELLS FOR BEGINNERS

Wand

BECAUSE I AM AWESOME and a Good God now.

> **!** Lie detected: you were NOT given the book (and by extension the wand) because you are "awesome" and a Good God now. Hyrrokkin said that you "still have far to go and a lot to learn".

Harrumph. I guess that's why I'm still stuck here...

Day One:
Friday

My name is Loki, and I am a hamster. Or I was until home time today. It all began yesterday (Thursday) with Thor being annoying. In class he was given a special prize for trying hard at his spellings: he was allowed to take the school hamster home. In case you don't know, this is a great honour among mortal children, akin to being asked to sit at the right-hand of Odin at a feast in Asgard.

Actually it's even better because hamsters are fluffy and cute and do not give long boring speeches.

Speeches? Me? I can't even speak!

After dinner, Thor placed the cage in his bedroom and while he was bathing his stinky mortal body, I crept in to watch the creature playing on its little wheel. It seemed to enjoy it. In fact, it appeared to be taunting me, telling me I could never enjoy such pleasures. That all the cool kids were hamsters. So...

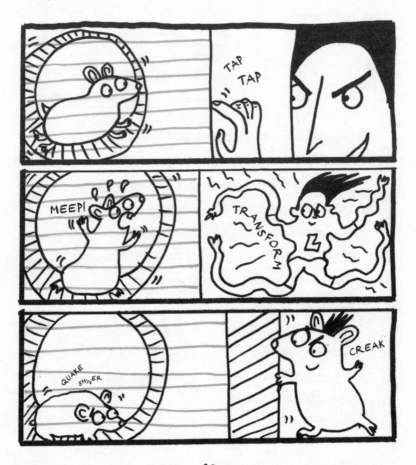

I played on the wheel and it was a delight. I gorged myself on seeds. I snuggled down in the warm shredded paper bedding. I sampled the many simple joys of hamster life, such as discovering that I had expandable cheeks and stuffing them with as many seeds as I could.

Unfortunately, Thor returned before I could turn myself back into mortal form, so I decided to hide until he went to sleep, to avoid having to explain myself. But I grew sleepy and snuggled down with the other hamster.

When I awoke this morning, I was still in the cage but I was no longer in Thor's bedroom. I was in our classroom at school!

ME!

(Class hamster cowering in corner)

Educational words that I could not see from my cage.

I was stuck. I couldn't transform until the classroom was empty, or I would risk revealing my godly powers to mortals. Again. (I might have got away with it once or twice, but I don't think Odin would see "getting out of a comfortable cage with a plentiful supply of food in order to show my teacher I actually *am* present, thank you very much" as suitably life-or-death.)

When the teacher left the room, I took my chance. But just as I popped open the cage door, another pesky teacher came in and proceeded to play on his phone for the rest of break.

Annoyed poos

HUMPH!

To my increasing frustration (and with an increasing pile of hamster droppings) I was not able to regain my human form until the end of the day. On the plus side, lessons are less boring when you can play on a wheel. Plus you can overhear gossip, as no one watches what they say in front of hamsters.

When one of the more observant classmates pointed out that there were now TWO hamsters in the cage, I had to hide under some sawdust for a bit. Luckily, someone else suggested that perhaps the hamster had given birth overnight. This story would not have stood up to scrutiny, as I was in the form of a fully-grown hamster. But, phew, another classmate interrupted the discussion by biting someone, providing a convenient distraction.

CHOMP

SCREAM

23

When the day was FINALLY over I escaped my cage, transformed, and ran home. Normally Loki runs for no one. But every second I delayed, Hyrrokkin and Heimdall would grow increasingly angry with me, and their rage is like the wolf that flies through the sky trying to eat the sun each day. At least the sun doesn't get nagged while it's being chased.

My fake parents, Heimdall and Hyrrokkin, were waiting for me. Thor was in the corner of the room, playing a computer game smugly. Thor manages to do EVERYTHING smugly. He even poos smugly. At least, I assume so. I don't watch him. No one needs to see that.

"I can explain!" I cried.

But, before I launched into my reason for missing breakfast and being "absent" from school, Heimdall gave me a hug.

"I was worried!" he said.

I blinked. Had a miracle occurred? Would I avoid punishment? Would everything be good and sweet and wonderful?

Spoiler: NO. No it would not.

After the hug came the shouting. So much shouting. As soon as Heimdall finished shouting, Hyrrokkin began. When she finally stopped, I explained that I'd been in hamster form and I had not, in fact, skipped school; I'd been in the classroom all day, even during breaks, which should surely get me EXTRA virtue points.

Instead I got more blame for "risking showing my powers", not telling anyone where I was, leading to people "worrying that you might be dead in a ditch" and, ludicrously, "hamster endangerment".

Then Heimdall got out some of his parenting books.

Heimdall finished his parenting lecture with my least favourite phrase.

Why can't you be more like Thor? He never causes trouble!

HUH. A bunch of dead Frost Giants would disagree with that. Well, they would disagree if they weren't dead because THOR KILLED THEM ALL.

After I pointed this out, I got sent to bed early for being cheeky. Did I perhaps hear Hyrrokkin chuckle? I don't know for sure because I was running upstairs from the wrath of Heimdall.

Day Two:
Saturday

LOKI VIRTUE SCORE OR LVS:

-50

Points lost for worrying your parents.

They're not my real parents!

In the morning all five of us went for some "healthy fresh air". This is Hyrrokkin-speak for walking in circles around the park at the sort of pace you'd usually expect of soldiers marching towards a battle for which they're very late. Personally, I don't know what's healthy about gasping for air.

MY LUNGS! They burn!

Shh, it's good for you.

Roughly 200 mph

Also, given that Hyrrokkin and Heimdall spent the entire time berating me, I began to suspect that this walk was actually a punishment in disguise.

As I wheezed, Hyrrokkin said to me and Thor, "Heimdall and I are going to do some vital research into a mortal tradition known as the holiday."

I already knew roughly what a holiday was, thanks to the definitions that appear in this book when I encounter a new mortal concept.

𝕳𝖔𝖑𝖎𝖉𝖆𝖞: when you travel across Midgard to another place on Midgard. Sometimes, this place is warmer than your customary abode and the aim of the holiday is to submerge yourself in the ocean like the Midgard serpent. Sometimes, the place is as cold as Jotunheim and the aim of the holiday is to throw yourself down mountainsides on skis like the Frost Giant Skadi. The purpose of every holiday is to make you forget that mortal life is brief, tragic and empty. Its secondary purpose is to escape those people in your life who you find tiresome.

When I expressed excitement at missing school, Hyrrokkin corrected me: Thor and I would remain behind.

AAA AHHHHH!

My thought process was confusing.

They are abandoning me because they find me tiresome!

No! I am a delight! They must be trying to escape Thor!

Yesssss, no parents! I can stay up all night eating crisps!

However, this hope was soon dashed when Heimdall chipped in.

"Odin's sending a god from Asgard to keep an eye on you while we're away..." His eyes shone, mouth twisting into an unsettlingly familiar vapid grin...

Oh. Oh no.

...you're so lucky...

Please no...

...to have someone so beautiful and charming taking care of you...

Not him...

Balder! My favourite brother!

Balder was EVERYONE'S favourite. Well, except mine. He might be sunshine and rainbows to everyone else, but he's always hated me for some reason.

> **!** **Could that reason be your personality and actions?**

RUDE!

Whatever his ridiculous and unjust reason for not liking me, he definitely has it in for me. When Odin swore to be my blood brother (long story, involves blood and a lot of crying on my part), Balder told him he would live to regret it. The cheek!

Everyone in Asgard always goes on and on and on about how amazing Balder is. Even Thor gives him The Look. Thor! The one who usually receives The Look from others! And Odin never shuts up about him! Personally I think he needs a slap.

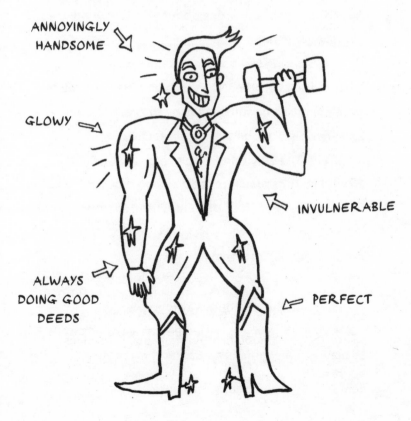

Not that I'd slap him. That would be pointless, as he's invulnerable, quite apart from the fact that I currently have all the muscular strength of a dead slug.

EVEN I COULD TAKE YOU!

"Loki, are you listening?" asked Hyrrokkin. Apparently, me fantasizing about punching Balder had not gone unnoticed.

"I was telling you both that Balder will *not* be here as Thor's brother. Mortal children require adult supervision, so he will be playing the part of Liam and Thomas's Uncle Bill."

Great. The only thing worse than having Balder around as Thor's perfect brother would be having him boss me around as my "elder" and "better".

! He **IS** your better. In every way.

I decided that the only way to make this horrifying curse of a situation bearable would be to play as many pranks on Balder the Irritating as I could fit into the days available.

	1	SWAP TOOTHPASTE FOR GLUE	WHOOPEE CUSHION	4	TOAD IN HIS BED	6
7	PRANK MESSAGE FROM ODIN	SNAILS IN HIS SHOES	DRAW ON FACE	PLASTIC WRAP TOILET	12	(REST)
FISH UNDER PILLOW	HIDE HALF HIS SOCKS	16	SHAVE ONE EYEBROW	18	ITCHING POWDER	20

> Need I remind you that playing pranks on Odin's favourite son does NOT constitute moral improvement, and that showing moral improvement is the only way you will be allowed back to Asgard? **!**

Diary, need I remind you that you are an enormous spoilsport?

When I answered the door, I hoped it would be Valerie and Georgina as we had plans for the afternoon, but it was only our stupid babysitter. Balder the Beautiful. Balder the Wonderful. Balder the Blah Blah Blah Can You All Shut Up About Balder Please I'm Going To Be Sick.

> **Correction: he did NOT say that. He said, "Hi Loki."** !

Yes, but his TONE implied he thought I was a worm. Anyway, then I invited him in very politely, even though he'd used a TONE on me.

> **Correction: you said, "Oh, it's you." Then turned around and walked back down the hallway, leaving him to invite himself in.** !

I think we can agree that Balder then came into the house. Everyone clustered around him in the living room cooing about how nice it was to see him. Well, not Hyrrokkin. Hyrrokkin does not coo. But she did slap him on the back so heartily that he nearly fell over, while Thor and Heimdall gave him The Look until I thought their eyeballs might fall out.

He looked at me!
He's noticed me!
I hope he still likes me!

Ugh. I hoped Valerie and Georgina would arrive soon so that instead of watching The Worship of Balder the Beautiful (yes, everyone REALLY calls him that), I could go to the cinema and watch a film.

Cinema: a building where mortals go to sit in the dark with strangers to watch films. Although in theory everyone is supposed to sit in silence, it is traditional for viewers to cough, sneeze and chew as loudly as humanly possible. Also, something mystical happens to popcorn, fizzy drinks and sweets that are on sale inside a cinema that makes them 10,000% more expensive than in normal shops.

Buy this and you will be bankrupt ↓

I looked at my watch. Or rather, at my wrist, as I do not have a watch. Linear time means nothing to a god. Except when it suits them because they want to escape from an unbearable situation.

"Oh dear, is that the time? My friends will be here soon," I said.

"Friends?" Balder asked. "Odin told me that Loki has found it hard to make friends."

I could not let that insult stand! "Odin said WHAT? Nonsense! I am very popular."

"I'm curious to experience this ... cinema," said Balder, after a pause. "So long as I can sit next to my beloved brother Thor!"

Thor wasn't actually invited, but if him coming meant I didn't have to sit next to Balder, then so be it.

I averted my eyes as they embraced. Such sentimentality makes me nauseous.

The word you're looking for is envious. !

"It's so nice to see brothers getting on so well," said Heimdall, smiling at this sickening display.

Both he and Hyrrokkin gave me a look as if to say, "Be nicer to Thor." But since they did not say it, it was easy to ignore.

"Now," said Heimdall, "Valerie's mums are picking you up soon. Has everyone been to the toilet?"

Heimdall has taken to asking this every time we go out. Just because of that ONE time when I had to get him to stop the car to urinate beside the road. Mortal bodies are so pathetic. And yet, mortal super-size icy SchlurpSchlurp drinks are so vast and delicious.

Sigh, that's better!

Valerie arrived with her mums – and also Georgina, my other very good mortal friend.

! Technically, she said you're only friends on a trial basis. You still have to prove yourself.

As the cinema is not far, we did more walking. (Hyrrokkin approved of this plan greatly. She thinks walking instead of driving makes you a better person, while I believe it just makes you a more tired person.)

While Balder walked up front with Thor and Valerie's parents, I fell in with my friends Valerie and Georgina.

"I didn't know your uncle was coming to stay," said Georgina.

"Neither did I," I said. "And I wish he wasn't. He's so..." I waved in Balder's direction.

(Valerie and Georgina are the only mortals who know our true godly identities. They are sworn to secrecy and unlike me, they have a habit of keeping their promises.)

"He's my pretend uncle. But he's Thor's ACTUAL brother," I said, with a sigh. "Now, enough about him. Who cares about Balder?"

"Thor does," Georgina pointed out. "Look at him! He's a big fanboy. I think it's quite sweet actually. My littlest brother's like that with me."

Thor was indeed trotting beside Balder as though being more than several inches away from him would cause him physical pain.

I rolled my eyes. "Everybody luuuuurves Balder."

"Except you, clearly," said Georgina.

"I try not to be into what everyone else is into," I said loftily. "I'm too cool for that."

"What other people think doesn't matter," said Valerie, agreeing with me like a good best friend. But, oh cruel betrayal, she did not stop there. "If I cared what other people thought, I wouldn't be friends with you," she went on.

Not cackling

Georgina cackled at that. I did not cackle.

During the film I shared my sweets with the others, to show Balder how good a friend I am. Annoyingly, he was watching the film and not my magnanimous gesture. So I cleared my throat before offering Thor a sip of my drink. Thor gave me a sceptical look.

After the film, while Thor, Georgina and Valerie were queuing for the toilets, Balder told me off for talking during the film. "Heimdall informed me that mortals prefer to enjoy their giant noisy screens in total silence. Perhaps to hear the sound of other people chewing better."

No wonde
they nee
a wee!

Thor was talking too!

"It's not Thor's behaviour that I am concerned with," said Balder. "You are the one Odin sent here to improve yourself – and as his loyal and obedient son, I am taking it upon myself to help you."

I showed him that I did not need his patronizing "help" by giving him a death stare. Sadly, causing death with my stare is not one of my powers. But in this instance, it was not for want of trying.

Balder gave me a very serious look in return with his frustratingly beautiful blue eyes. "I will be hard on you as I help you be better."

You may hate me at times.

I was about to point out that I hate him ALL the time but he went on before I could.

"But trust me," he said, folding his arms and looking down his nose at me, "everything I do will be for your own good, in the long run. I am not here to be your friend. I will not shy away from my duty, ordained by Odin, nor will I spare your feelings in pursuit of my goal. You see, I am here to change you from a villain into a hero."

"I'm not a villain!" I objected. "I'm a Good God now!"

You are a terrible monster made of filth and horror. If I saw you on my shoe, I would wipe you off.

Correction: he did not say that. He said, "Now, go and wash your hands, they have popcorn sugar all over them."

YES BUT HE SAID IT WITH A TONE.

That evening, while Heimdall cooked a dinner of roast meats, potatoes and carrots, I noticed that Odin had issued Balder with a mobile phone to use during his time on Earth. He'd left it on the kitchen sideboard. Oh, Balder. You are too trusting.

Easy to guess Passcode

43

During dinner, there was a ring on the doorbell.

"Who could that be at this time?" asked Heimdall, getting up to see.

"Frost Giants!" growled Thor, also rising.

Hyrrokkin put a hand on his shoulder and pushed him back gently into his seat. "Frost Giants may not be the wisest of all giants, but even they do not telegraph their attack by ringing the doorbell."

Thor grunted, somewhat disappointed. Just then...

"But… but…" stammered Balder. "I didn't summon that young man! I don't even know what that foodstuff IS!"

As Heimdall apologized repeatedly for his inferior cooking and Balder denied ordering a takeaway, Thor began to tuck into the pile of pizzas. He never lets social awkwardness get in the way of eating.

As Balder blushed and stammered, a slow grin spread out over my face. "Not such a Good God now, are we, Balder?" I said. "What an ungrateful guest you are! How RUDE to insult Heimdall's food like this!"

That, I now realize, was my mistake. Pulling a beautiful prank should be an end in itself. It's the gloating that always gets you caught.

LOKIIIIIIII!

I sighed. Still. It was worth it to see Balder's face.

"Go to your room!" said Hyrrokkin. I skipped up the stairs chuckling at my witty trick.

Until Odin showed up in my bedroom.

"Hey!" I squeaked. "Haven't you heard of knocking?"

"I have existed since the dawn of the world. I INVENTED knocking," said Odin. "But you should not be making jokes. Hyrrokkin told me what you did to Balder. I am, to put it mildly, displeased. Balder is my beloved son and this is NOT the way to gain my favour."

I scrunched up a bit smaller on my bed, hoping that my mortal puniness would make Odin less angry. To my surprise, he sat down on the bed beside me.

"You appear to have forgotten why you are here on Midgard, Loki," he said. "Allow me to remind you." He reached behind him and produced a snake. "You are here as a punishment. You are here to become a better person. If you succeed, your reward is Asgard."

If you fail...

"An eternity of snake torture in a dungeon?" I finished. "Ah yes, how could I forget?"

"The choice is yours, Loki," said Odin. "Do better, and come home one day. Or..." He gestured to the snake. "Snakes are still on the table."

He released the snake into the air, where it disappeared.

SNAKELESS

47

Odin's such a show-off.

"Understand?" he said. I understood. "Good. Now go and apologize to Balder."

Then he disappeared.

POU

I trudged downstairs. Heimdall, Hyrrokkin and Thor were in the kitchen, but Balder was in the living room, sitting in an armchair, as if he were waiting for me. I stood in silence for a moment, gritting my teeth and wishing for death rather than this humiliation.

I looked at my feet, as though they were the most bewitching and entertaining objects in the world.

Loki. It's unlike you to be lost for words.

IRRITATINGLY MUSICAL VOICE

"I'msorryIorderedpizzasonyourphone," I whispered, without looking at Balder.

Balder looked at me, his perfect face an inscrutable mask. After several eternities, with a couple of ice ages thrown in for good measure, he finally replied.

"Loki. I accept your apology," Balder said, nodding to me slightly. "Now perhaps you should apologize to Heimdall for hurting his feelings, like a Good God."

I went into the kitchen. I apologized to Heimdall. And then I went to bed because humiliating suspense is tiring and unpleasant.

"Sweet dreams!" Balder called up the stairs after me, his voice dripping with sugar and spice and all things incredibly irritating.

Day Three:
Sunday

LOKI VIRTUE SCORE OR LVS:

-100

Points lost due to pizza prank. Making Heimdall sad is NOT a virtuous act, nor is framing Balder for insulting Heimdall's cooking.

It might not be virtuous, but it WAS funny.

When I went to sleep, I had a very sweet dream. I dreamed Balder fell in the sea and was attacked by a sea monster.

At breakfast, no one mentioned my prank, but Thor ate leftover pizza while giving me suspicious looks. I think it was his way of telling me he was watching me. Well, that and the fact he said, "I'm watching you, Loki. Leave Balder alone or ELSE." Subtle hints have never been Thor's particular strength.

As he poured us all orange juice, Heimdall put on a bright, cheery smile.

"We're going on holiday first thing tomorrow, so I thought we could spend the day as a family," he said.

"Oh no, I cannot lower myself to spend time with this fiend," said Balder.

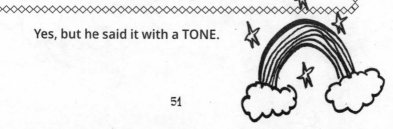

I spit on his soul and scorn his measly physical form, which is a pale shadow next to my magnificence.

Correction: he actually said, "That sounds lovely. It is surprisingly nice weather for this time of year in this region of Midgard!"

Yes, but he said it with a TONE.

For our family activity, Hyrrokkin decided that we should try a mortal game known as paintball.

Paintball: mortals who live safe lives go to the woods and dress as soldiers and shoot one another with guns because they do not experience enough pain and danger on a daily basis. The bullets only contain paint so no one dies. Odin finds this frustrating, because all who die nobly in battle come to Asgard to join his army, which he will need at the end of the world in Ragnarok.

I do sometimes think the definitions in this book are not 100% objective. Unlike Odin, Thor decided he LOVED paintball.

DIE DIE DIE DIIIIIIE.

Actually, it's dye.

THWICK!

I did not love paintball. Those little balls are HARD and my buttocks lack cushioning.

Halfway through the game, when I was thoroughly dead, Balder came over to me and said, "I'm glad you're dead, you are a disgusting and insignificant wretch and you deserve both death and eternal snakey torture!"

> **Correction: in fact, he said, "You have paint on your nose."** !

Yes, but he said it with a TO—

> **Loki. Give it up. You're only wasting your own time replying to me.** !

Later, when I'd showered all the paint from my bruised body, I wandered into the garden. Heimdall was putting piles of dung onto the plants while talking to Balder. This felt like a perfect opportunity to research how best to pull a prank on him.

So, I transformed myself into the worm he clearly thinks I am and went over to listen for clues. I didn't like what I heard.

"Letting him believe he can become good isn't fair. It's giving him false hope. Some people just cannot be saved."

I gasped a tiny worm gasp. So he wasn't actually seriously here to help. He probably just wanted to prove to Odin that I'm bad! The snitch!

"You haven't been here, Balder," said Heimdall. He was shaking his head. "I've seen Loki change. Yes, he's a mixed bag. But I believe there's good in him."

My little worm heart clenched at the last part.

"Hmm," said Balder. He fixed Heimdall with his bright blue eyes. "A person is either good or bad. There's no in between. If a fruit is partly rotten, the whole fruit is lost. And I fear Loki has rot in him."

"He might surprise you," said Heimdall. He shrugged, breaking away from the laser blue of Balder's gaze.

Balder nodded, then patted Heimdall on the back, heartily. "Very well, Heimdall, I trust your judgement. You are wise and pure of heart."

At that, Heimdall smiled so widely that I worried his face might split in two and the top of his head would fall off.

Thank you, dear Balder.

> I will give him a chance, and root out the rot, even if it is an impossible task.

So, he doesn't think I can be good! His TONE was real! Hoity-toity too-good-for-me Balder thinks I'm going to inevitably end up evil! RUDE!

I wriggled away and transformed in private. I needed a new plan. Playing pranks on Balder wouldn't be enough. I'd have to show him that I could be good. Prove him wrong. That'll make him look silly, won't it?

! **Need I remind you that you're ALREADY supposed to be doing virtuous deeds?**

I know, I know. But now I will be doing them AT Balder. That'll show him for thinking I'm bad!

! **So you'll be doing more virtuous things but only in order to spite Balder? This is going to make calculating your virtue score incredibly fiddly.**

GOOD! I live to make you suffer.

! **Well, that just made calculating it a LOT easier.**

TURDS.

Day Four:
Monday

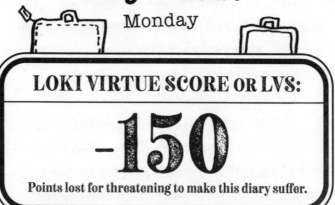

LOKI VIRTUE SCORE OR LVS:

-150

Points lost for threatening to make this diary suffer.

Heimdall and Hyrrokkin were up early with their bags, ready to go. They were going on a type of holiday known as a cruise.

Cruise: when ageing mortals sail around in a large boat that stops off briefly at various landmasses. The aim appears to be to have a rushed, stressful glimpse of many places rather than staying in one place and actually exploring it properly.

Can't stop! 900 more places to semi-visit.

MEEP!

"Now, make sure you do what Balder tells you,"
said Heimdall. "And if in doubt, do what Thor does."

"Yes, I shall burp and fart and eat like a starved
piglet, of course," I said.

"Don't be cheeky," said Heimdall.

"I cannot be Loki if I cannot be cheeky."

Heimdall laughed at that. (See, Balder, everyone
adores me, I am charming.) I gave Balder A Look
– not THE Look – just to make sure he'd noticed.
Annoyingly he was chatting away to Thor like the
unobservant handsome oaf he was.

"Don't forget to practise your spells," said
Hyrrokkin. She'd given me a spell book and Thor had
given me a wand, and, admittedly, both objects had
spent the time since then gathering dust in my room.

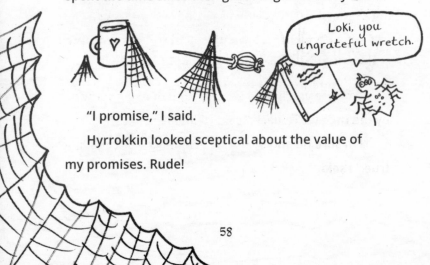

Loki, you
ungrateful wretch.

"I promise," I said.

Hyrrokkin looked sceptical about the value of
my promises. Rude!

"And you must do your chores and walk the dog and feed my snakes," she added.

"Yes, yes of course," I said, wondering the best way to trick Thor into doing all of those things for me.

"And at school, make sure you don't give in to peer pressure," chipped in Heimdall. "I read about peer pressure in a book called *Your Child Is Weak and Easily Led*."

Huh. Nice to know Heimdall thinks of me as weak! Very supportive of my fake father.

"I'm sure you'll both be very fond of one another by the time we're back," said Heimdall.

"I'm sure he and everyone else will ADORE me, it is true," I said.

"I have created a family chat so we can all keep in touch," said Heimdall.

 **The Smith Family Chat**

> [Heimdall has added Thor, Hyrrokkin, Loki and Balder]

> Balder: Hi…

 [Loki has left the chat]

But Heimdall just added me back again, so I shall accept my fate … for now. In any case, perhaps it will offer me a chance to show my sunny and winsome personality to Balder. I added some emojis to demonstrate the purity of my own heart.

When they'd gone, Balder announced he would be walking us to school. I was about to say "No! Never!" when I realized it would be a good opportunity to further charm him and demonstrate

what a lovely and wonderful person I am. I started off by talking to him about the time I defeated a group of Frost Giants and saved the world.

He told me to stop showing off.

As I was trying to think of a conversation topic that would live up to Balder's ludicrously high moral standards, he turned to Thor.

"Having met Loki's friends – all two of them – I am looking forward to seeing all yours, my brother. Tell me, shall there be many waiting at the school gates to welcome you?"

Thor blushed. "Oh, you know. I have many friends. But not close ones that get excited about seeing me."

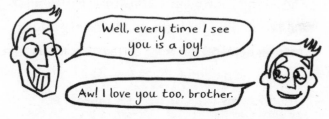

Well, every time I see you is a joy!

Aw! I love you too, brother.

For once, I was delighted to arrive at school so that I didn't have to listen to this inane chatter any more. In fact, I even listened to the teachers in assembly for once. And – what do you know – for once they had something interesting to announce.

The play was called *The Wicked King and the Good Prince* and it was about – can you guess? You'll be shocked, I tell you, shocked and surprised by the truth! – a wicked king and a good prince.

The title suggested to me that it was not going to be a subtle and nuanced theatrical masterpiece. When I discovered that the drama teacher had written it herself, I knew for certain that it was going to be beyond dreadful.

And yet, my heart soared. My time for stardom had come. All would see how truly glorious I am.

As the best actor in our class, nay our year, nay our school, nay Midgard, I would of course play the lead role of the good prince, thereby forcing Balder to admit I am, indeed, a very good person. Perhaps he would even do so in some very public way?

I WAS WRONG, LOKI IS A
TRUE PARAGON OF VIRTUE
love Balder

The drama teacher then told us that the auditions
would be tomorrow lunchtime and that an anonymous
school benefactor was donating costumes and money
for proper sets and all kinds of props. We could even
have a LIVE horse onstage. Well, a small pony.

At that moment I thought Valerie and Georgina
might break the sound barrier with their screams of
joy.

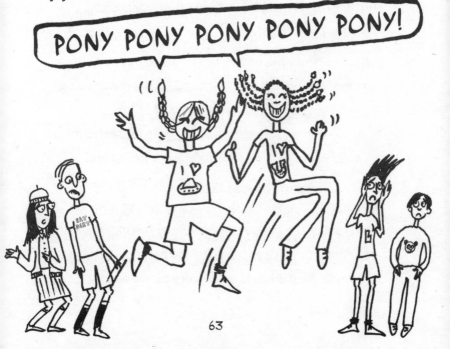

PONY PONY PONY PONY PONY!

I couldn't help wondering why someone would give money to a school when you could spend it on something useful, like a speedboat or an in-home cinema. But I was glad Valerie and Georgina were excited about the play too.

> **!** Can I detect you ... caring about the feelings of other people?

No! I mean. Maybe. Do I get points for it?

> **!** Yes. But you lose the same amount of points for asking for points just for demonstrating "human" feelings.

In Art, Valerie asked me what part I was going to audition for. I gave her an incredulous look.

"Oh, I won't have to audition. I am a tremendous actor with a very handsome face." I leaned in closer.

Plus, I'm the god of lies, so acting is like breathing for me.

Ms Loach said that everyone has to do an audition. That's how it works. Also they don't know you're the god of lies and you're not allowed to tell them.

I waved away these objections. "Ms Loach cannot deny my talent. She will give me the main part. What do you want to be?"

"I don't mind, as long as I get to meet the pony," said Valerie. "Plus, it'll be fun doing a play with you and Georgina and Thor."

"Thor? Thor can't act! How will he get a part in the play?" I said.

Valerie shrugged. "He's really good-looking and popular, so I think it's basically in the school rules that he'll get a big part."

I was about to demand to see these ridiculous rules when I realized she was joking. It's sometimes hard to tell with Valerie.

That evening, Balder insisted that we have dinner together as a family rather than watching TV while eating on our laps. I wasn't allowed any crisps before it either. The majority of the items on my plate were GREEN. During this poor excuse for a meal, I decided to prepare Balder for my triumph.

Not crisps

"There are auditions for the school play tomorrow and I expect to get the lead as the good and handsome prince."

"If they're looking for someone good and handsome, they should cast Thor," said Balder, glancing up from his meal to smile at his beloved brother.

I hope not. It would take time away from me playing football.

But Balder wasn't having any of it.

"Being on Midgard is a gift, brother." He got up and gestured enthusiastically with his almost comically muscular arms. "Do as I am doing and try everything! Experience life! Push yourself outside your comfort zone."

Thor looked sceptical but he listened. Apparently Balder's enthusiasm was infectious. Like the mortal disease smallpox.

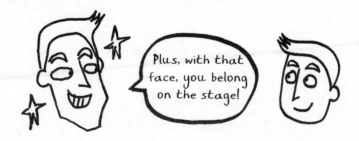

Plus, with that face, you belong on the stage!

It was like they were in some kind of secret handsome club. Except it wasn't secret because I was standing right there!

Thor's doubts evaporated in the beaming light of Balder's enthusiasm. "You're right. I should try new things – I shall audition with all the confidence I feel playing football!"

I decided that I would go and do some magic, as that is something I can do and Thor cannot. So I went upstairs, got out my wand and dusted it off, then opened the book to a random page.

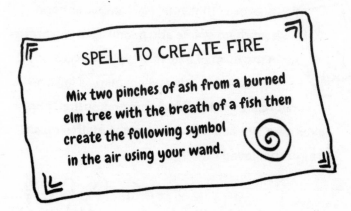

SPELL TO CREATE FIRE

Mix two pinches of ash from a burned elm tree with the breath of a fish then create the following symbol in the air using your wand.

I shut the book again. That sounded like a lot of hard work. I had assumed spells would just be something I would be able to do right away, since I am so clever. But apparently they require preparation, effort and repetition. Tiresome! I'll stick to animal transformations, thank you very much.

A GIANT'S GUIDE TO MAGIC SPELLS FOR BEGINNERS

! You promised Hyrrokkin you'd practise them. The point of practising is you don't start out good right away, you get better.

Maybe that's true for most people. But I'm always instantly good at things! Unless the thing in question is stupid and pointless and ridiculous.

I decided to play on my phone instead. I've discovered that you can make videos and post them online and people give you praise in the form of hearts. People seem to find it especially amusing when animals fall over, so I called Fido to my room and pushed him over then videoed it and set his downfall to music. The internet loved it!

Huh?

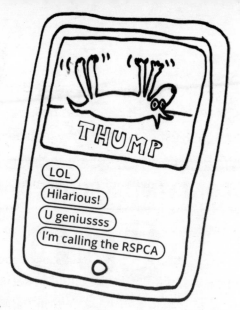

Mostly.

But just then Balder came in and told me to get off my phone.

"You're not on Midgard to have fun," he said. "From now on you will only be allowed computer time for homework and you can have no more than half an hour of screen time on your phone, in which you can reply to essential messages such as the family chat, or politely converse with your severely limited number of friends."

I hate Balder. He is an evil tyrant who must be stopped.

Or must be persuaded I am delightful... I can't decide.

Day Five:
Tuesday

LOKI VIRTUE SCORE OR LVS:

-200

25 points deducted twice for a) making a mockery of Fido on the internet and b) giving up on your magic practice so quickly.

S **The Smith Family Chat**

> Hyrrokkin: Morning everyone! How are you doing? Our cruise is going well. Only ten people have had food poisoning so far, which is apparently better than last year.

> Heimdall: I bought myself a flimsy hat made from straw on board. It appears to be an important mortal tradition to purchase such items.

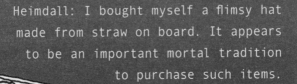

Balder: Very fetching, you handsome dog!

Heimdall: Thank you! x

Hyrrokkin: How are you, Loki? Are you doing your chores?

Balder: He is not. Luckily, I enjoy washing up and cleaning in general and the house is spotless.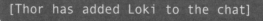

 [Loki has left the chat]

[Thor has added Loki to the chat]

Thor: Also he made me walk the dog and feed the snakes.

 Loki: Ahem, you mean I gave you the opportunity to spend quality time with some excellent animals!

Hyrrokkin: WALK THE DOG AND FEED THE SNAKES TODAY LOKI OR ELSE! And do the washing up!

71

I washed up the breakfast dishes and walked Fido before school AND fed the snakes. How's THAT for virtue?

! **You only did it because Hyrrokkin threatened you.**

OK, OK ... but, in Maths, I did a truly virtuous thing...

I turned to Valerie at the end of the test and told her of my amazing act of heroism.

"Oh. Right," she said, sharpening her pencil.

She didn't even give me a round of applause or tell me how proud she was to be my friend. Honestly, being good is so thankless!

Well, I'd soon have a way to prove to everyone – especially Balder – that I come across as a very good person. At lunchtime, we had the play auditions. I read the hero's big speech. I was, if I say so myself, brilliant.

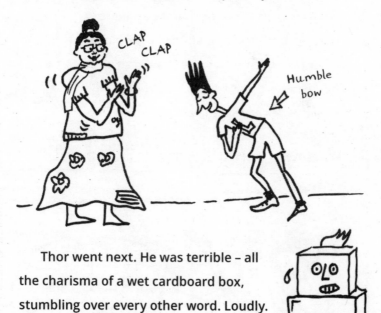

CLAP
CLAP

Humble
bow

Thor went next. He was terrible – all the charisma of a wet cardboard box, stumbling over every other word. Loudly.

BLAH
BLAH
BLAH

Valerie went after that and she was surprisingly good. Her singing is terrible, but she's got a certain powerful presence on the stage and was genuinely intimidating as she read the part of the head jailer. Georgina was good too. She read the part of the witty warrior princess and was very funny!

And, might I just say, I have truly grown as a person in one short month as, before, I was jealous of Georgina! Now I can glory in her triumphs. As long as she doesn't take the main part that I want. If she does I will fill her pencil case with spiders.

! **What were you saying about making moral progress?**

This is the **THEATRE**, darling. It's kill or be killed.

In any case I shan't have to resort to anything like that because I was fabulous and the main part of the handsome princely hero is already clearly MINE.

After school I was in such a good mood that I had another go at practising my magic. The ingredients called for elm bark so I went to find an elm tree but it turns out all the ones near here have died out since the spell book was written, so I gave up.

Quitter! !

Hey, it's not my fault that the elms got a stupid disease! And soon I will be so busy playing the hero onstage that I won't have time to do any spells anyway, so I might as well wait until Hyrrokkin gets back. I bet she'd rather we did them together.

That's generally not what someone means when they ask you to practise while they're away. !

I'll practise tomorrow. Are you happy now?

At dinner, Balder made us say one thing we were grateful for that had happened that day. He started us off by saying he was grateful to be able to spend so much time with his dear brother Thor. I said I was grateful that I'm such an amazing actor and will inevitably get the main part in the school play. Balder said that wasn't really in the spirit of gratitude and turned to ask Thor what he was grateful for. Thor said he was grateful that the auditions were over and that he was now certain the theatre was not for him. I agreed a little too heartily and Balder said I wasn't allowed pudding and made me go to bed early.

Day Six:
Wednesday

LOKI VIRTUE SCORE OR LVS:

-150

Points gained for resisting the temptation to cheat.

I arrived at school feeling joyful. Even Balder scolding me at breakfast for calling Thor a Human Fart Factory could not spoil my mood.

Our first lesson was Drama. Even on an ordinary day, that's my favourite lesson. But today was special. Today, the teacher was announcing the cast of the school play. I pictured the moment that everyone would see my name next to the role of the heroic prince.

But then stinky reality came and dropped a huge turd on my dreams.

For a start, the teacher didn't even put the parts up on a dramatic list, so everyone just had to gather around Ms Loach as she announced them. I felt cheated even before I found out who'd been cast.

As she read out the roles, it got worse. So much worse. The WORST.

But I'm good now! Doesn't she know this? Surely my audition showed that I could be a glowing and heroic and sympathetic character?

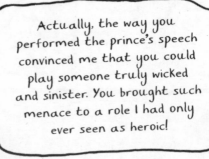

Actually, the way you performed the prince's speech convinced me that you could play someone truly wicked and sinister. You brought such menace to a role I had only ever seen as heroic!

And what did Thor bring to the role of hero? The ability to fart loudly on command?

When the drama teacher noticed I was displeased, she said that it was a compliment to be cast as the villain, as it's the most complex part. But if it was such a compliment why were the rest of my class clustering around Thor like flies around a ripe and rotten corpse?

I listened to the rest of the cast being announced while trying to hold back tears of pure, howling rage.

- Valerie – Warrior Princess Brunhilde
- Georgina – Warrior Princess Gudrun
- Margot – Court Jester
- Nouria – Guard
- Lottie – Warrior Maid in Waiting
- Milan – The Prince's Page
- Charlie – Head Jailer
- Fierce Boy One – Chief Guard
- Gus – Wise Wizard

Valerie and Georgina talked about their parts in the play over lunch and I waited for them to ask me about mine. Couldn't they tell I was suffering from inner turmoil? So insensitive.

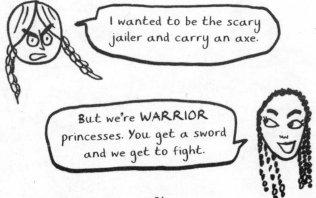

I wanted to be the scary jailer and carry an axe.

But we're WARRIOR princesses. You get a sword and we get to fight.

"I just don't want to marry a prince," said Valerie.

Georgina grinned, "Don't worry, the princesses get married to each other."

"Oh," said Valerie, thoughtfully. "That's alright then! Phew."

"Also ... there's a pony!" said Georgina.

"If we get a scene with the pony then I'd happily play a singing tree," said Valerie.

This is a very bold claim. Valerie *hates* singing.

"A scene with the pony would be the greatest thing to happen in my entire life," said Georgina.

Valerie nodded in agreement.

I wasn't listening. I was feeling sad and hoping they would guess. How could they go on about something being amazing for them when it's bad for me?!

"Aren't you going to ask me how I feel about being cast as the villain?" I prompted, when it was clear neither of my alleged friends were going to psychically understand my pain. What monsters!

Georgina shrugged. "Sure. How do you—"

"So … you're not happy about it then?" said Georgina.

"But," said Valerie, "it's the part that's onstage the most and has the most lines, and you like people paying attention to you."

"And talking," added Georgina.

"But I'm GOOD now!" I pointed out. "It's an insult, casting me as a villain and Thor as a hero! She's saying Thor is better than me!"

"That's not how acting works," said Georgina. "Acting is pretending."

"Yes, but casting *does* work like that! Casting is when someone looks into your soul and tells you your true essence," I wailed.

I feel like theatre must be really different on Asgard.

"Look, you really should take it as a compliment," said Valerie. "Ms Loach always gives the best actors the villains' parts. I heard that one person who was cast as the villain in one of her plays went on to be a famous Hollywood actor."

"Who?" I asked.

> Dunno, I'm not very interested in actors.

Well that was useless.

On the way home, Thor congratulated me on being cast as the biggest part. I couldn't tell if he was mocking me with his victory, so I made sure to put one of the dead mice we use to feed Hyrrokkin's snakes into his shoes when we got home, just in case he deserved it.

Stinky

Even stinkier

Balder was very excited when he heard we were both in the play.

> Thor! You are the perfect handsome hero! Everyone will adore you, as they should!

"Loki, how convenient that you don't even have to pretend to be evil! You can express your true nature onstage in a manner that harms no one!"

Why does everyone think I'm bad?

I'm good! I'm GOOD! *I'M GOOD!*

> How about instead of just saying you're good over and over, you do something good to demonstrate it?

But I've done lots of good things already. You mean I have to do MORE?

> Yes. Every day.

Well, that is unacceptable! What kind of good things can I possibly do EVERY DAY? It is not as though babies are lying around needing to be saved from wolves on a daily basis, is it?

> It doesn't have to be something dramatic. Just steady acts of good. Congratulate Thor on his success. Help Balder make dinner. Even practising your magic, like you promised Hyrrokkin, would count. Fulfilling promises is a good act.

FINE!

So I got out my wand and the spell book. I practised one of the less complicated spells. It helped you conjure an illusion that you'd washed your hair when you hadn't and required you to mix the song of a lark (I found a clip online) and the whisker of a mouse (having a supply of frozen mice to feed Hyrrokkin's snakes truly is a blessing).

Let the grease slide away and my hair shine like the dawn

It didn't work.

GREASE →

LACK OF SHINE →

STILL AWESOME THOUGH

You tried the spell once. That's not practising!

I practised it one whole hideously unpleasant time! Then I threw my wand across the room because it was clearly broken and went downstairs to find a snack.

Balder told me I wasn't allowed a snack because dinner was almost ready.

Balder hates joy. Balder hates life. Balder is the worst.

Except ... he IS the best cook, I'll give him that. But that's the ONLY reason he's the best in any way and all the other gods are wrong about him being the best.

Even my hat is handsome.

Day Seven:
Thursday

LOKI VIRTUE SCORE OR LVS:

-200

You gained points from practising your magic a
little but a greater value has been deducted due to
the dead mouse in shoe incident.

Spoilsport.

I walked the dog AGAIN and fed the snakes and no one
even reminded me to do so. I demand that you give
me the points I am due!

> I'd be more inclined to give you points if you
> didn't demand them so rudely.   !

OK, OK! I demand you give me the points I am due
... please?

I'll confess I actually enjoyed walking Fido.

Although he is currently a mere dog and not a wolf, he appears to know that I am very important and wonderful and handsome. Or at least, that's what I believe his frequent tail-wags mean.

I have a slightly more uneasy relationship with the snakes. On the one hand, one of my children is a giant snake, but on the other, Odin frequently threatens me with an eternity of snake torture.

You wouldn't torture me for all eternity would you?

Notsssss iffff youuuu feeedsssss usssssss miiiiiceesssssss.

We had a rehearsal at lunch. You know what's worse than Thor getting your rightful dream role in a play? Thor getting your dream role in a play and being terrible at reading his lines. I mean, it should not come as a surprise that this lout would be bad at uttering basic mortal phrases. He is not a god who is known for his way with words. He is mostly known for his way with hammering giants into a squishy pulp.

Meanwhile, I read beautifully and am busy learning all my lines and all HIS lines. Well, it's my duty as an actor. If Thor were to have a nasty accident, I'd be ready to step in, nobly and selflessly, to save the show!

After school, Balder said he'd help Thor with his lines. They spent all evening together practising. It's so unfair! Thor's getting all this extra attention for being bad at something. I don't get extra attention for being bad! I get snakey punishment threats!

Well, not EVERYONE was ignoring me at least. Hyrrokkin sent me a postcard from her holiday.

Postcard: a mortal tradition wherein a person on holiday sends a card featuring luxurious and beautiful images to show that they are having a wonderful time and the recipient is not. Usually includes a phrase such as "I wish you were here" when, in fact, the opposite is true, as they have gone on holiday to escape you.

Dear Loki,

We submerged ourselves in the sea at our last port stop and we have made friends with another mortal couple. Apparently making friends on holiday who you never plan to see ever again is an important mortal tradition. I hope you are practising your magic and being good for Balder.

Love from Hyrrokkin xx

I have not shown our address so my legions of adoring fans cannot find me.

92

My guts felt like they were twisting in on themselves
when I thought about not having practised my magic.
My conscience had something to say about that.

> Guilt. That's guilt you're feeling.

Well, I don't like it. What can I do about it?

> You could try practising your magic?

But practising my magic didn't make me feel any
better. It just made me feel angry because the spell
failed. Now I feel guilty AND annoyed with my stupid
magic book and my stupid wand.

Day Eight:
Friday

> **LOKI VIRTUE SCORE OR LVS:**
>
> # -150
>
> Points gained for practising your magic.

Points are meaningless to me today! I am full of woe because I cannot escape this stupid play! I thought I was safe for a while but in English, the teacher announced we'd be studying the script. I pointed out I didn't need to study it as I already know it off by heart. Mrs Williams said learning things off by heart didn't mean you understood them. Thor gave me a smug look at that point. In unrelated news, he later found a large wad of chewing gum on his seat and had to go and get spare shorts from the lost property cupboard.

Mildew smell

But even after that the play *still* followed me! At lunchtime, we were summoned by the drama teacher to the school hall, where there was rack after rack of clothing, as well as several piles of assorted objects, ranging from fake swords to hats.

"The costumes have arrived!" she said, as though announcing the arrival of a divine being such as myself rather than some mouldy old clothes.

Georgina's eyes were full of a desperate kind of hope, as though she awaited news of whether her parents had returned safely from a long and dangerous sea voyage.

"No, she'll only be coming for the performance itself," said the drama teacher.

Georgina drooped. "Awww, Ms Loach," she complained.

But Valerie whispered to her that at least they could go and pick out swords and crowns today, which cheered her up.

"I *would* look good in a crown," said Georgina. "And you DO love swords."

"You really would," said Valerie. "And I really do."

The teacher told us to pick out costumes that suited our characters. "I'll give you free rein!" she said.

At least, she said that until the girl playing the court jester decided to dress as a panda, and Mrs Loach wrenched back creative control. So I was denied even the crumb of pleasure that would have been choosing my own outfit!

"You, Liam, should be dressed all in black. With a moustache," she said.

Now, while I can pull off ANYTHING, it was a somewhat tedious costume. What is it with mortals and thinking that wearing black makes you a villain? Wearing black merely means you'll get completely covered in hair if you come into contact with any kind of mammal.

KEEP THAT WHITE CAT AWAY FROM ME!

I needed something else to really make my costume zing. I rifled through the prop piles and found a glinting ring. Perfect! It had a red stone that looked like a ruby. It was probably plastic, but it had a lovely shine to it. I slipped it on my finger and finally I felt right. I tried out a villainous laugh.

Mwahahahaha!

Everyone turned around and looked at me, impressed. OK, while I want everyone to know that I'm a good person, I have to admit, I did not despise the attention I got for being stylishly, handsomely evil.

"I knew I chose the perfect villain!" said the drama teacher, clapping her hands.

You look every inch the foul fiend!

Well, that ruined my mood. She clearly DID pick me for the villain part because she thinks I'm evil! How dare she?

When we put away our costumes, I kept the ring. It was so shiny! Also, I was annoyed at the drama teacher and stealing something from her made me feel a bit less cross.

! You're going to lose points for stealing.

Worth it! That'll show that bad-choosing teacher that I should have been the hero.

! I do not think it will show her that.

Valerie came around after school to play computer games. Only Balder said we weren't allowed because I was permitted to use the computer only for homework. I pointed out that the punishment wasn't meant to apply to Valerie, and Balder pointed out that I was a snivelling wretch who should be grateful he's allowed to sleep in the house, never mind use the computer.

Correction: he said, "Stop trying to twist my words, trickster." !

OK, but he said it with a TO...

NO HE DID NOT. !

Anyway, instead of computer games, we played a board game about murder in my room.

As we enjoyed some wholesome murder and violence-based entertainment, Valerie said she liked my ring.

> Thanks. An old friend gave it to me.

! LIE DETECTED.

Yes, but I didn't lie to YOU so you don't need to correct me.

! Perhaps not. But I DO feel a strong urge to subtract points ... on top of the points you lost for stealing it in the first place.

"Isn't it pretty?" I held my hand up to the light, watching the ring glint on my finger. "I thought I might wear it for the play."

"I'm not very into jewellery but it definitely suits you," said Valerie.

"Valerie, everything suits me," I pointed out.

She didn't reply. She was clearly too impressed with my shiny ring to speak.

Downstairs, I could hear Balder and Thor practising lines again. "It's so annoying that Balder's spending all this time with Thor. It's like they've got this stupid club for handsome people."

Not that I'm not handsome of course.

"Maybe it's nice for Thor to have his brother here," suggested Valerie, failing completely to comment on my handsomeness. "It's not like he's got any close friends."

"But he's got ME here," I pointed out. "Why would you want another brother or a close friend? Plus, he's popular, which is more valuable than having close friends!"

Valerie had nothing to say to that, so I'd clearly won the conversation.

Loki
10

Valerie
0

And Valerie Kerry falls at the last hurdle, Loki is VICTORIOUS, this is the best performance in competitive conversations I've ever SEEN! Stupendous work!

JUDGES

When Valerie went home, I went up to my room. Just then, I heard a voice.

Valerie is wrong. Thor should be clamouring to spend more time with you. As should Balder. You're the one who matters. You should be the hero in the school play. You ARE good. You are a hero.

I was confused for a moment and wondered who was speaking. Then I realized, of course! It was my conscience!

! Loki, I do not think it was your conscience.

Wait a minute. Didn't Heimdall tell me to listen to my own conscience and not fall for peer pressure telling me what to do? What is this diary if not a peer?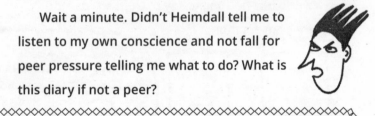

! Odin is not your peer! You are inferior to Odin!

That's exactly what someone trying to apply peer pressure would say! They'd try to make me feel bad about myself so I'd do something bad.

> That's not it. I have a bad feeling about this! I do not believe it is your conscience speaking! I do not know who it is but I do not like it! **!**

I'm going to bed!

But I decided that, before I went to sleep, I would watch the ring sparkle for a while. It was so very beautiful.

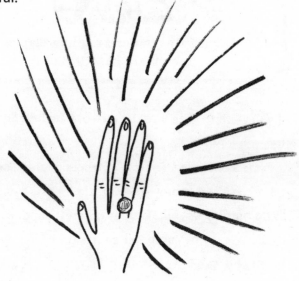

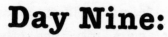

Day Nine:
Saturday

If you want to gaze into the face of true horror and terror, picture this:

It is a Saturday. The day of freedom and glory for all children. A day when it is their right and duty to do nothing useful. This day is reserved for such things as playing computer games until your eyes bleed and watching television shows that your parents or guardians deem unsuitable because of all the stabbings and rude words.

SWEARING
AND SHARP
OBJECTS

On such a day, just imagine my disgust and horror when Balder got me out of bed at an offensively early hour and informed me that today we would be joining a school-based "Family Fun Day".

Let me repeat that. He wanted me to go to SCHOOL on a SATURDAY! THE HORROR!

It gets worse. This "Family Fun Day" at (*spit*) school involved sportsball.

WOW! That scares me and I'm a horrifying slime monster.

Balder said it was because he hated me and wanted me to suffer.

So basically he's saying my suffering is my own fault! Rude!

So I was cruelly forced to put on sportsball clothes, which are like my normal clothes but made of an unnaturally shiny fabric that clings to your body like a disgusting sucking leech. Balder packed a "delicious healthy picnic" and off we went.

But I grudgingly admit it *was* delicious, despite being healthy. Somehow that makes it worse because it makes him correct.

On the way I used up a few of my precious moments of screen time messaging Valerie, because I am a very good friend.

Are you coming to the ridiculous Family Fun Day? I need someone to share my suffering!

No, sorry. I'm going to a pony party at the stables with Georgina!

I began to type "I hope a very large pony steps on your foot as a punishment for abandoning me" but I deleted it and just sent some friendly emojis, because I am a Good God now.

When we arrived at the "Family Fun Day", I discovered that there was going to be a parents versus children sportsball match. This cheered me.

Surely the ancient ones would allow their spawn to win, humouring and coddling their little feelings?

But no. I was wrong. It turns out that when you encourage middle-aged mortals to engage in feats of sporting prowess, they become monsters who seek victory at all costs, even if it should be the cost of their own children's pride and/or limbs.

Worst of all, I was cruelly forced to participate in a running race between the adults and the children. I will gloss over where I came in this farce...

! You came last.

I hate you. The key point here is that the race resulted in a draw between Thor and Balder. I thought this would lead to recriminations and fisticuffs but, in fact, they both laughed and congratulated one another. All the adults and children gave them BOTH The Look.

108

It was sickening. Mortals are so easily impressed. I mean, no one even congratulated me for not cheating! I could have so easily! I could have turned into a rapid animal such as a gazelle and reached the finish line before anyone else. But I didn't! Because I'm GOOD NOW.

> **Correction: in not cheating you are achieving the bare minimum moral level of "not being bad". There's a difference between that and being actively good.**

PAH!

When I got home I loitered in my bedroom. Due to Balder's ridiculous and unjust screen time rules, I could not play with my phone and had to find other entertainments. At first I spent time drawing great art.

Looking up from my masterpiece, I spotted the ring with the red stone on my bedside table. I thought that, to create objects of great beauty, it might help to wear a beautiful object, so I put it on and got back to drawing.

As I drew, I heard a voice.

What happened today was a disgrace! You deserve The Look from everyone! You deserve to be as beloved as Thor and Balder.

I decided that this eminently sensible, wise and factually accurate voice had to be my conscience. Perhaps my conscience had a slight cold, which was making it sound different?

Self-delusion detected.   **!**

Then I heard the voice again.

You should wear that beautiful ring next time you have an important endeavour ahead of you. For luck.

I rubbed the ring on my finger, feeling the edges of its stone, and felt comforted. I *did* deserve a little luck, it was true.

> **When mysterious disembodied voices talk to you, you should proceed with caution and scepticism.** !

HA! Says the disembodied voice of the very-often-mysterious god Odin.

Day Ten:
Sunday

I went to the park with Valerie in the morning. I am
of course above such childish pursuits as playing
on the swings and going around and around on
the roundabout. However, since my best friend is
actually an eleven-year-old mortal child, I must
humour her whims.

> **As this doodle shows, you clearly know deep down that you do NOT merely play in the park for Valerie's benefit, so I shall not offer a lie correction. But I will suggest you reflect upon why you feel the need to pretend you are above such things.** !

Reflecting is for losers!

> **Sigh.** !

Like I was saying, as I humoured Valerie, I told her my woes from the so-called "Family Fun Day".

"Everybody is so obsessed with Thor," I sighed. "And now they're obsessed with Balder too. When, by all that is just and right, they should be obsessed with me."

Valerie thought about this for a moment. "Popularity is a weird thing. I know I'm not popular but I never think the most interesting people are the popular ones."

Maybe being popular doesn't matter at all.

I laughed at her naivety. "Valerie. I have only been on this mortal plane a few months but I can already tell that being popular is of paramount importance."

"Why?" asked Valerie, clambering to the top of the slide.

This was an odd question. Being popular is so obviously important – based on everything I have seen of mortal culture. But it was very hard to think of reasons why that might be the case. It was one of those mortal truths that defied logic. Such as "peanut butter tastes better when scooped out of a jar using your finger" and "school lessons towards the end of the day feel 9,000 times longer than ones at the start".

FORBIDDEN DELICIOUSNESS

"I don't know why it's important," I admitted, as she zoomed to the bottom of the slide. "But I have observed that most mortals crave it."

As the greatest of all the gods I should have everything that mortals crave!

WHOOOOSH

> **Correction: you are NOT the greatest of all the gods and you get exactly what you deserve, plus I hope you only said that in your head, not out loud for any passing mortals to hear!**

"The more I think about it the more I think it is my right to be popular," I went on.

"I don't think it works like that," said Valerie. "I think it's usually the best-looking people who are good at sports that get to be popular."

"What about the best-looking people who are good at acting?" I said.

"Oh, I'm not sure. Maybe?" said Valerie, appearing to give this some serious thought. Not that Valerie thought about anything un-seriously. I once asked her whether she'd rather lick the inside of a dirty dustbin or the bathroom floor, and she thought about it for a good five minutes before answering. (Apparently it depends on whose bathroom and whose dustbin.)

Once she'd considered the matter of popularity, she said, "I think being good at acting can make you popular when you're a grown-up and famous? But being in a school play can't."

Well, I can't wait to become a grown-up and famous. I must be popular NOW!

I can't make that happen. But if you like you, could come to the mall with me and Georgina and her friends from her class?

"I don't really want to go," Valerie continued, "but Georgina says her friends say she's been ignoring them, and she said it would be good if I met them. So I've got to go. It might be less boring if you come to the mall too?"

While I know that my presence makes every occasion full of thrills and joy, I have to admit it was rather nice to hear Valerie Kerry, best friend of Loki, say it out loud.

"Excellent plan," I said. "Let us go to this mall!"

Mall: a brightly lit, cavernous mortal temple containing many shops which sell things that you neither want nor need. In a mall it appears possible to get your ears pierced at every turn. It is also a place small children come to get lost and weep for their parents.

Balder gave me permission to go to this mall with Valerie, Georgina and her mysterious other friends. Not because he thought I deserved fun, of course. No, he saw it as an opportunity for me to improve myself morally.

It will do you good to spend time with others and not make everything about you.

What a fool. For Loki, spending time with others provides an audience for my magnificence. I do not intend to think of them at all! However, I will receive their praise and gratitude for my presence, which will no doubt be mine as soon as they set eyes on me.

I wore my ring so that I would make a good first impression. Disappointingly, when I first arrived none of these strange girls paid me any attention whatsoever. Until I heard a voice ... the voice of inspiration!

Popular people touch the arms of people they're talking to in order to make them feel special.

I do not think that is the voice of inspiration. !

I decided to test out the wisdom from this mysterious and yet clearly benevolent voice, and approached Georgina and the girl she was talking to.

"Hi Loki," said Georgina.

"Greetings," I said. "And who's your friend?"

"This is Sophy, from my class," said Georgina.

"Charmed," I said, taking her by the hand.

Liam,
isn't it?

"Are you OK, Sophy?" asked Georgina, looking at her friend with concern.

Why was she looking at Sophy? Didn't Georgina know all the cool people gaze upon ME these days?

Sophy nodded at Georgina, not taking her eyes off me. "You didn't tell me you were friends with Liam Smith," she said.

I didn't think it really needed an announcement.

"You've heard of me?" I said to Sophy, blushing a little. Perhaps my fame was already spreading, as the (very handsome) true star of the school play?

"You're only the most interesting person at school! And mysterious!" said Sophy. Her eyes had an odd sheen to them, as though she was looking very far away. No doubt too shy to look me in the eye, given she was so in awe of me. "You're so amazing and cool," she went on. It was excellent.

Georgina, looking unsettled, took Sophy by the arm. "Let's go and look at the bookshop," she suggested, dragging her friend away and glancing back at me.

I watched them depart, smiling with great satisfaction. My attempt to become popular was bearing surprisingly rapid fruit.

Valerie came over to me from where she was lurking. "That was weird."

"I think Georgina's friends already love me!" I said.

"I ... are you sure?" asked Valerie.

"This is me we're talking about! Why would you doubt that all should worship me?" I asked, frowning.

"Well, based on ... evidence and ... how people usually react to you," said Valerie, "it doesn't seem that likely."

Since Valerie was going to be like THAT, I decided to strike up a conversation with another of Georgina's friends, shaking her hand as I had done last time, as it had clearly proved charming.

"Hi, I'm Nouria," she said, and we fell into happy conversation. Well, I happily talked and she happily listened as though everything I said was fascinating. Which, given that she is a mortal and I am Loki, the most silver-tongued of the gods, is highly likely. Especially because I was talking about the most fascinating topic in all the nine worlds: moi.

> **I don't know why those girls were so interested in what you had to say, but remember, mortals are fickle and "popularity" means nothing compared to true friendship.**

I've already GOT true friendship with Valerie and the beginnings of one with Georgina. I would like some fake and shallow popularity in addition!

Anyway, I had a magnificent time. By the time Balder was due to pick me up, I'd spoken to all of Georgina's friends, and now they were all my friends – nay, perhaps even my worshippers.

Unfortunately, after a while, Sophy and Nouria blinked and then looked at me a little oddly, as though they couldn't quite place me. I put it down

to insecurity and nerves. After all, it's hard to be
a hanger-on, I'm sure. You never know if you are
worthy of the truly popular people!

> **I urge you not to chase shallow popularity.
> That is NOT the path to virtue.** !

Yes it is! Being beloved by all means I am worthy!
Honestly, for a diary containing all the wisdom of
Odin, you really are very dull-witted sometimes.

> **Well, we both know that comment will be
> reflected in your next virtue score...** !

In the evening, Balder inflicted a new horror
upon me. After what he claimed was my "poor
performance" and "slightly worrying lack of fitness"
at the Family Fun Day, he decided that I needed to
build up my strength. Despite only having been on
Midgard for a week or so, he has already bought
various instruments of mortal torture. Like all good
torturers, he showed me the instruments first
before he used them on me.

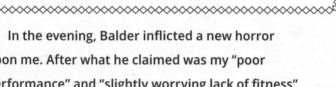

I am almost too tired to write this diary tonight.
I am a shell of a being. Everything hurts. I may, in fact,
be dying.

! **Correction: you did one minute on the rowing machine and lifted the lightest possible weight five times.**

Can't reply ... too weak...

Day Eleven:
Monday

LOKI VIRTUE SCORE OR LVS:

-300

Points deducted for insulting the intelligence of the Allfather's diary-based simulation.

In Maths, I had an unusual experience: I got top marks in the test. Odd, considering that I didn't know any of the answers and just wrote down any old nonsense that came into my head.

They weren't even numbers for the most part.

1: Sausage

2: Belly button fluff

3: What is the answer? Who knows? Who cares? All is death.

4: I hate maths

5: 283483748374 9247 and a half

When the test was over the teacher collected our papers...

Mrs Williams gushed in praise of me. Now, I have to confess, for a moment I did think perhaps something was off, given my answers. Then I came to wonder ... perhaps I understand mathematics on a level so profound that it transcends numbers? Perhaps sausage *is* a true expression of a complex mathematical concept?

Perhaps the source of the true fundamental harmony of the universe *is* belly button fluff?

I suspect you were somehow cheating. Hmm. But HOW?

!

I did nothing! Other than answer the questions!

Later that day our teacher set us a new project. We're studying Vikings and we have to build a longship. (Modern mortals sometimes think "Viking" means everyone from a particular time in history who lived in northerly places. Actually, being a Viking was more of a job title.)

WANTED: VIKING!

Duties include: sailing, raiding coastal towns, looking fierce.

The ideal candidate: works well in a team, very little sense of self-preservation, likes violence, doesn't get seasick.

Salary: a split of the plunder, depending on experience.

Now, I was frequently on Earth when the Vikings were around so, in theory, creating one of their ships should be a doddle. After all, we're talking about the people who worshipped the very ground upon which I trod! They were my greatest fans!

> **!**
>
> **Correction: your name didn't actually come up that often in the prayers of the people of those regions, except to say, "Loki, please stop messing with my crops" or, "Loki, please don't make Thor angry, I can't handle these constant thunderstorms and lightning – all my trees are charred stumps now."**

Ahem. No comment.

As I was saying, I was frequently on Earth among the people of the Nordic regions at that time but I can't say I paid a great deal of attention to their ships. Technical details have never interested me so, all in all, I have a vague notion that Viking longships were ... well, long. And full of Vikings. And probably floated on water. But beyond that my memories are faint and vague. Irritating. I'll just have to copy Thor's project.

Sails... maybe? ↓

Oars?

128

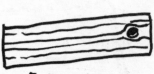

↖ Probably wooden

He was always obsessed with technology when it could be used to fight people.

After school we had rehearsals for the play. I was, of course, line-perfect and full of charisma. Thor remembered about half his lines and kept standing in the wrong place and messing everything up for everyone else. He doesn't deserve that part. It should be mine!

It's true. You are under-appreciated by so many fools.

I was pleased to hear the soothing voice again. I decided it didn't matter what the voice was, precisely.

I suspect it does matter...   !

Oh go and eat your own pages, stupid book.

Day Twelve:
Tuesday

LOKI VIRTUE SCORE OR LVS:

-400

Points deducted for cheating on the test although I do
not yet know how you did it. A magic spell you're not
telling me about? I will find out eventually...

I'm telling you about ALL
my spells. I get points for
practising, remember? Why
would I leave them out?

! Hmm... then I suspect it may be related to the
mysterious voice you keep hearing...

At break, some of my fellow pupils were playing a game called Bulldog that involved one group of children running at another group of children and, by touching them on the arm, forcing that child to join the opposite team. No one asked me to play and I might have accidentally left my foot in the path of one of the running children. But in my defence, I helped them up afterwards!

My charisma is clearly powerful, as the person I tripped invited me to play afterwards. However, they appeared to have become a little confused about the rules.

They were giving me The Look! They weren't chasing me because they wanted to capture me! They just wanted to be close to me! But I dislike running, so I told my fans to chase people on the other team.

Soon there was only one person on the other team, and it was Thor. So I sicced my army of children on him. It was beautiful.

Afterwards, I regaled the assembled crowd with my amazing victory. They hung on my every word!

Valerie had kept trying to get my attention about something during the game but I ignored her. Doesn't she understand how important it is for me to give my fans my attention?

It turned out she'd hurt her foot and needed someone to take her to the nurse because she couldn't put weight on it. Hasn't she heard of hopping? She's so needy sometimes.

In Science, she initiated a very strange conversation. She asked me if everything was OK and if there was anything I wanted to tell her. It was very odd, as everything was more OK than it usually was. I was finally getting some of the adoration I deserved! I told her it was a science lesson and we should focus on doing science. Luckily, Valerie likes science so I was able to distract her with the growth of mould on a bunch of bananas.

After school, the family chat group had a flurry of activity. I didn't bother checking it at first but, after the fifth ping, my curiosity was piqued.

Hyrrokkin: I hope you are all well.

Hyrrokkin: Our ship was attacked by Frost Giants.

Balder: Oh no! Are you OK?

Heimdall: We were swiftly victorious and managed to convince the other mortals that the frost that had descended upon the deck was the result of a malfunctioning ice dispenser.

Balder: Thank Odin!

Hyrrokkin: We sent them back to Jotunheim duly humiliated!

Thor was too furious to reply. "I can't believe they fought giants without me!" he raged.

"It is good to sometimes go without the things we like," said Balder. "It only makes you morally and emotionally stronger, brother."

I gave Thor a superior look. "I am clearly better than Thor, as I am not at all upset about missing out on fighting giants."

"No, Loki. You're not better. You're just a lazy coward who flees from any and all physical conflict," said Balder, in a chilly voice.

<hr />

! **Correction: he did not say that last sentence.**

Well, he implied it with his TONE!
Balder went on.

> Thor may lack self-control, but he is noble and brave and kind.

That wasn't fair! I have virtues! I have so many virtues I can barely contain them within this feeble mortal frame! For example, today when we were playing the chasing game in the playground, I gave my fans all the attention they required! I'm so kind!

<hr />

! **Correction: showing off does NOT count as a good deed.**

In any case, I decided not to point out how very virtuous I am. Balder's facial expression made me think he'd take it the wrong way. When he gets angry, he doesn't look grumpy like Heimdall. He looks suddenly like he's sculpted out of ice or stone. It's MUCH scarier.

"Now." Balder's face thawed. "Let's work on your lines."

Surprised, I said, "Oh, well, I don't actually need your help—" But I confess, I felt a glow in my cheeks at the idea that Balder was warming to me.

However, Balder had already turned away from me, arm around Thor's shoulders as they took themselves off to a corner of the sitting room.

As I said. I didn't need his help.

I went and read a book. Balder might claim the internet is full of "evil things", but mortal books contain just as many horrors.

The Evil Clowns Who Come and Eat Your Face At Night

Day Thirteen:
Wednesday

Unfortunately, the book gave me nightmares. I blame Balder. If I'd had my phone, I would've looked at pictures of kittens instead!

I kept waking up screaming, so no one in the house got much sleep.

Walking Fido this morning, yawning my face off, I discovered that, when I threw a stick, he would bring it back to me. For some reason this utterly pointless activity was pleasurable. It felt, for a moment, that the world was in balance.

But then I had to go to school. I was too tired for school, so I told Balder I should get the day off because Fido would miss me too much.

Unfortunately Fido went and licked Balder's ankle and curled up at his feet, the traitor.

So, school it was.

In Drama, we had a lesson with Georgina's class so we could rehearse the play. It was a bit of a squeeze in the drama room and everyone kept bumping into each other.

But something odd happened. The more I was jostled against people, the more everyone seemed to cheer up. Even when I accidentally pushed the teacher over, she praised me for my amazing acting skills!

Liam, you should seriously consider a career on the stage. Or the screen. I have never seen such talent in one so young! Not even the famous Hollywood actor I taught. She was nothing compared to you!

And when I did a monologue about my plans to do evil and destroy the good prince, the entire class fell completely silent and then applauded afterwards. FINALLY! People are getting it. I am amazing! I realized my problem before had been that everyone loved Thor because the only opportunity to show off was in sportsball. But now we were doing a play, it was my time to shine. And I basked in the warm glory of their Looks.

Valerie and Georgina came over to say I should be playing the main part instead of Thor. It is good that I have such wise and correct friends. You should always surround yourself with smart people, I feel. No dullards in my friendship circle!

(Except for Thor, but he's hardly a friend. More of an unwilling housemate.)

After school, we had another rehearsal in the hall. The jostling of the smaller room must have been what created that wonderful theatrical energy because this time, everyone paid attention to Thor – a sure sign they'd lost the plot.

BLAH BLAH BLAH BAD ACTING BLAH

Then I heard a voice. My conscience?

This isn't how things should be, Loki. Not how things should be at all. You need to change this.

But how? I went home feeling very sorry for myself. If only I could MAKE people like and appreciate me all the time. I heard that voice again.

I will tell you, when you are ready.

Honestly, my conscience can be quite annoyingly vague sometimes. Plus, it can't make its mind up. Because, after that, it said – sounding slightly different...

Don't listen to that voice. Your goal should be to be good, not to be universally beloved.

I take it back. I liked the vague thing it said better.

After dinner, Balder took Thor off on a trip, leaving me all alone.

"We're going to help out at a food bank," he explained.

Food bank: in the mortal realms, many people have more food than they could possibly eat. Others do not have enough. Instead of merely sharing out food more evenly in the first place, the people with large amounts of food leave extra food in places called food banks, where people without food can collect supplies.

143

I waited for him to invite me too, just so I could turn him down. But he appeared to be waiting for something. Perhaps for me to beg for an invitation? Loki does not beg.

Eventually, he looked a little sad and shook his head. "Well, I suppose it will just be me and Thor then." And off they went.

Leaving mortal children alone is probably illegal, but I chose not to report him because I am kind and generous.

! **Lie detected.**

OK, fine! It was because I realised that being alone meant I could play as many computer games as I liked. I don't know why Balder is so obsessed with screen time being bad. I didn't move or look away from the screen for four hours while I played and I feel great!

Day Fourteen:
Thursday

LOKI VIRTUE SCORE OR LVS:

-550

Points deducted for ignoring the opportunity
to volunteer at the food bank.

But he didn't ask me!

**The point of charity is that you do it willingly
without being asked!** !

Today we engaged in the mortal ritual known as a
school trip.

Wheeeeee!
Freedom!

School trip: when teachers transport their pupils to a museum, zoo or other place usually reserved for leisure and spoil it by making the pupils do schoolwork while they could have been enjoying themselves. Parents and guardians must agree to this by signing a piece of paper known as a permission slip, so that if the children die while on the trip, the teachers will not be held responsible.

My whole year went, so the teachers had lots of pupils to not kill.

Balder spent so long making Thor a very special packed lunch with hand-crafted pasties filled with delicious meats that he barely had enough time to shove some mouldy snot sandwiches in a bag for me.

! **Lie detected. He gave you the exact same lunch.**

Well, I bet he spat in mine!

The trip was to a Viking museum and, when we arrived, I took great pleasure in telling Valerie and Georgina how it would no doubt be 100% the story of me, Loki. It would be a song in praise of my greatness!

A poem to my glory! An epic tale of my many wondrous deeds!

When we got inside, I was met with crushing disappointment. Every display we passed was *Thor this, Odin that!*

There was ONE measly display devoted to me, Loki, greatest of all the gods and, let's just say, it was NOT flattering.

LOKI WAS BAD NEWS! WHAT A BAD PERSON HE WAS! PLUS NO ONE REALLY WORSHIPPED HIM ANYWAY BECAUSE HONESTLY, WHY WOULD YOU? LOOK AT HIM, THE LOSER.

That's not EXACTLY what it said.   !

I'm paraphrasing! That's an important skill we learned in English class. It means taking something waffly and long and making it succinct and pithy.

Well, they *should* have said more about me, shouldn't they? I'm LOKI for Odin's sake! I mean, for MY sake!

While I was sulking – I mean, contemplating the fact that I had been wronged by a great injustice of museum labelling – Valerie grabbed my arm and pointed to a cabinet. The display barely mentioned me, so I don't know why she thought I'd be interested.

"Look," she said. "That ring looks just like the one you have!"

She pointed at a display called "ANDVARI'S CURSE". It had a little notice with a picture of a ring in it.

Eerily similar!

Norse mythology tells that a dwarf called Andvari put a curse on a ring after Loki took it from him. This curse destroyed everyone who possessed it, driving them to do terrible things to the people around them, including those closest to them.

Oh, THAT ring. OK, yes, I admit, that whole curse business was a little bit my fault. But I didn't know the dwarf was going to curse the ring! (Long story – involves an otter, a dragon and a woman in a ring of fire – tell you later. Much later, as it doesn't reflect all that well on me, as stories go.)

I thought of my ring, nestling safely at home on my bedside table. Yes, perhaps in certain lights you could say they looked similar. But, don't all rings look a bit similar? Well, all rings with red stones look like all rings with red stones. And besides, I think that ring was probably destroyed.

There is no record of this destruction in Odin's memory. !

Well, Odin doesn't know EVERYTHING does he?

I told Valerie it was definitely a different ring.

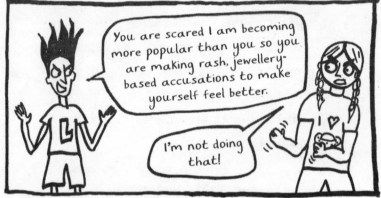

I told her not to take such offence at someone merely stating the truth. She did not like that either.

"If we're talking about telling the truth, then I'm not sure that what you're experiencing is popularity," she said. She was clearly lashing out, poor thing.

"Nonsense! My fans can't get enough of me!"

"Well I can."

Valerie stomped over to a group of girls with Georgina at their heart. They started trying on fake armour and giggling.

I considered going over to them. But I felt a little sad all of a sudden that I didn't have my ring with me. I don't know why. Probably because then I could have held it up next to the picture of the ring to prove it was definitely a completely different not-cursed ring.

Anyway. If it *was* a cursed ring ... nothing bad is happening. Only good things! So what kind of fool would call that a curse? A BLESSED ring, maybe.

Some other pupils were looking at a display that was dedicated to Thor, who stood nearby.

"Nah, he's rubbish," replied the heinous infant. "He can only turn into horses and stuff. Thor can summon lightning and kill giants."

I felt a wolf-like fury build inside me. I wanted to tear and rend and rip. How dare they? I AM THE GREATEST! Thor is nothing!

Oddly, though, Thor shifted uncomfortably from foot to foot before walking away, muttering something that sounded like, "This is incredibly embarrassing."

(Surely I misheard and he, in fact, said, "This is very *pleasing* because I am the best and everyone is saying I'm the best.")

"Odin's interesting too," said another child. "He has ravens and he's in charge. It'd be good to be king, you know?"

Well, I thought, I'm just as wise as Odin. And just as powerful as Thor. But with much better hair.

Also, I AM the king in the play and stinky Thor is only a stupid prince. So what if he's a good prince? What's so good about being GOOD?

BIGGER
because
KING

A mere
prince

> **Being good is very important and you know that. If you want to get back to Asgard one day, it is essential. You do WANT to get back to Asgard, don't you?** !

Yes! But I've been good for MONTHS and where's it got me? Valerie's accusing me of being cursed and Thor's getting all the attention.

Except... I *have* been getting more attention lately. Just not all the time. I need more! This part-time popularity thing is unacceptable! Perhaps if it was full-time, I wouldn't *need* to go back to Asgard. I could be happy here instead! If only everyone adored me all the time.

> **!** **Loki, no. That's ... that's not the lesson you should learn here.**

When I got home I put the ring on. It felt comforting as well as very pretty.

I heard my conscience whisper to me...

You can have all the adoration you require.
I promise. One day ... sooooon...

> **!** **Correction: Loki, I seriously do not think that is your conscience.**

I'm putting this diary away. It is stupid and I am sleepy. GOODNIGHT.

Z
z
z
z

Day Fifteen:
Friday

LOKI VIRTUE SCORE OR LVS:

-550

Holding steady, but I sense clouds gathering. Clouds of evil. And it has something to do with that voice...

In English class, we learned about something called an unreliable narrator. That's when a book's written from the point of view of someone who doesn't tell the truth to the reader or even to themselves, sometimes.

Obviously I am a reliable narrator. Because this diary points out every tiny fib.

Reliable

I've given up on the tiny ones. And the lies you tell yourself and believe. And some of your exaggerations.

!

Well, that's on you. Anyway, I don't have to lie to myself to make myself feel better because my life is amazing right now! I actually *enjoyed* a PE lesson. I realize this sounds unnatural but let me explain:

I was getting changed for PE and the teacher told me I couldn't wear jewellery to play sports, so I tucked the ring into my sock. I had to keep it safe, after all. Looking after valuable things is what responsible people do!

My mysterious-yet-helpful-and-clearly-virtuous voice agreed.

High security storage

Keep it safe. It would be bad to lose something so beautiful. And you don't want to be bad, do you?

! Correction: That voice is NOT helpful or virtuous. I don't know yet for certain what it is. But I'm starting to suspect.

Don't be ridiculous. I'm crossing out your nonsense.

! Doesn't make it untrue. I suppose you'll have to find out for yourself. The hard way.

So, anyway, I went to PE, ring safely tucked away. We played football – yes, I'm calling it football not sportsball, because finally it deserves a name of its own. For I, Loki, god of Asgard, am finally gaining recognition as the genius footballer I truly am!

It might be true that, during the match, I accidentally kicked my fellow players many times instead of the ball, fell over, and missed every goal. But everyone else seemed to think I was amazing and that's what matters.

I politely declined their offer as being a football captain sounds like hard work. But I did find it pleasing to bathe in the glow of their adoration. However, my joy was short-lived. After the match, Thor started doing tricks with the ball and everyone gathered around him, forgetting about me, their great football leader, in a matter of moments. Humanity is so fickle!

The thing is, Loki, while Thor is there, you can never truly shine. Not for long.

On the plus side, Thor's triumph did not last long, as the football had a little accident involving a rusty nail I found at the edge of the playground and Thor had to cease his silly little ball tricks.

OOPS! MY BAD.

Day Sixteen:
Saturday

That wasn't me.
That was the nail.

Lie detected!   !

So, in more important news, I hate Thor. He lives to
torment me and spoil my fun. While walking Fido
this morning, he accused me of using a spell to make
everyone think I'm good at football. He didn't believe
that I could have suddenly become so skilled. The
cheek!

It is not cheek. You have **NOT** become more skilled. You just fooled everyone that you had.

Ah, but *he* doesn't know that!

I could have been practising my ball skills in secret!

Or you could have been practising MAGIC in secret and cast a spell on our class.

I felt an ever-so-slight twinge of guilt when he said that. I had NOT been practising my magic for many days now. But I ignored the twinge. It was a silly twinge.

"Everyone still thinks you're good at football, you know. You don't have to worry," I said to Thor. Which I think was very kind of me.

"That's not the point," growled Thor. "I know I'm good at football. But I also know you're NOT and something fishy is going on."

But when we got back home, a miracle happened. Thor told Balder his theory. And instead of taking Thor's side like the pair of annoying handsomeness twins they are...

Balder smiled at me a little sadly. "Yes you do, you pathetic worm. I don't believe you can ever change. You're scum. You're the lowest of the low."

> **!** Actually, he said, "Be honest with yourself, Loki. Or you'll never truly be able to change."

His words may have been saying that. But his TONE...

> **!** SIGH.

I went to brood for a while, away from Awful Balder and Annoying Thor. But brooding alone is no fun because no one can see how sad you are. So I came downstairs again to find them in the garden.

Were they doing anything worthwhile? They were not. They were messing around with bits of wood. Tedious. I had no desire to do anything so strenuous.

"Would you like to join us?" offered Thor. "We're making a Viking ship for that school project. You could make yours with us?"

"No. I would never use Hyrrokkin's tools without her permission," I said, quickly. Luckily I am very virtuous now and it is a superb way to get out of hard work.

The day got better, however. I went to meet Valerie and Georgina. This time Georgina's classroom friends agreed to come to the stables instead of the mall. The classroom girls did not appear pleased with this turn of events.

Valerie told me and Georgina about a riding competition in which she intends to participate.

Valerie giggled. Presumably it was the nervous giggle of someone living in fear of public humiliation.

"I shall absolutely *not* embarrass you with my support," I declared, proving how good I am for not wishing to shame my friend.

Valerie did not laugh this time.

Sophy, meanwhile, sighed rather loudly, then commented, "Horses are so BORING. And gross. It totally stinks around here. We should've gone to the mall."

"*Sophy*, that's really rude," said Georgina. "No one forced you to come."

Thinking of something → horrible to say

Annoyed ↓

Upset ↓

I realized this was an excellent opportunity...

> **To side with Georgina against the mean mortal child and stand up for your friend?** !

No, silly! To break the tension by making everything about me, me, me!

> Stop what you're doing and look at me, for I am glorious.

The ring flashed.

> My power grows. I no longer need contact.

I wondered for a moment who was speaking. Never mind, I thought. The most important thing was that everyone was gazing upon me adoringly. Except Valerie, who was screwing up her face like this.

Meanwhile the others fawned on me, just as they should. "I don't mind boring horses when someone as cool as *you* is around," said Sophy. "Georgina, your new friend Liam is the literal best. He's *so* cool."

Intense concentration

"SO cool," agreed Georgina, gazing upon me in wonder. As it should be! I am wonderful!

But when Valerie flicked her on the arm, she blinked, then looked at me with a new, less pleasant expression.

He's doing something to us, isn't he?

Yes. If you focus on something that's not him, you can stop it. I focused on my favourite alien conspiracy theory.

RUB RUB

Georgina screwed up her face in furious concentration. "I'll think really hard about that tricky bit in my trumpet piece. I'm thinking about the arpeggios... Ooh, I think my head's clearing. I no longer want to tell Loki how cool his hair is."

Well, I did NOT like this development one little bit.

"Loki, you need to stop whatever you're doing," said Valerie. "It's not OK!"

"You're being creepy," said Georgina.

The voice whispered to me again.

These two might need more of my energy. Rub the ring. Focus on the ring.

I did what the ring said. (Yes, OK, I knew it was the ring. I'm not stupid.)

Valerie and Georgina were now gazing at me with rapt attention, just as I deserved. I went home happy, with everyone doting on me and listening to me like I was the most fascinating person in the world. I mean, I AM the most fascinating person in the world, so they were merely behaving appropriately. Now, even Valerie and Georgina were wrapped up in my charm, not able to snap out of it as the ring's power grew. All was good with the world! I was on top of the world!

I shall RULE the world!

No! Loki, you're in trouble. Big trouble. If I had a physical form I would be on my knees begging you to call Odin now and ask him for help.

That feels unnecessary. Everything is perfectly fine! In fact, it's wonderful!

> **It is NOT wonderful. That ring is CURSED. Curses can never be used for good. They always end up hurting people.**

Shhh. You just don't want me to be happy. And, saying NEVER to me, to Loki, the god of rebels, the god of not doing what I'm told ... well, that only encourages me!

The ring spoke to me again.

Good, Loki, good. You're almost ready.

"Ready for what?" I asked.

To make my power eternal, you need to do something for me...

"Anything!" I said. Then, after a moment's thought. "Well, anything that's not difficult or requiring of great effort."

You must ignore your diary's puny prattling. It wants you to be a coward. To go running to Odin. You want to be brave, don't you? Not cowardly, like Thor and Balder think you are. You want to be brave.

I want to be loved.

I can make that happen. Just wear me. Listen to me. Do as I say.

Yes, yes, I will.

Well, that's enough diary-writing for tonight. Big yawn. Sleepy now.

Loki! Don't listen to it! !

Loki? You've gone to bed, haven't you? !

I hope you're not still wearing that ring... !

Day Seventeen:
Sunday

LOKI VIRTUE SCORE or LVS:

-700

Many, many points deducted for listening to a
ring that even you acknowledge to have powers.
This is bad, Loki. This is VERY BAD.

I don't like you.

! **I am not here to be liked. I am here to speak
the truth.**

I slept long after the sun had risen, and when I finally
awoke, I felt strange. So I stayed in bed, despite Thor,
Balder and Fido making enough noise to raise the
dead in Hel.

Balder called me for breakfast but I pretended not to hear. Then Thor came and farted on my head so I was forced to get up so I didn't die of the foul fumes.

"You're very quiet this morning," said Balder once I was downstairs and safe from the emanations of Thor's putrid bottom.

You should be quiet and humble more often. You are too often arrogant and loud.

171

I just nodded. I felt quite far away, as though I was merely looking down on this puny mortal body, and heard the ring speak.

You are more than this. You are not a mortal. You are a god. You deserve greatness. What do you desire most?

Across the table, Balder was beaming at Thor and Thor was beaming at Balder. "I cannot *wait* to see you play the hero," Balder was saying. "So fitting! It must be frustrating for you down on Earth, pretending you are not a mighty god to these mortals."

"Mphh mph mpph," said Thor, shovelling toast into his face.

"At least, for the night of the play, all shall see you as the hero you are," said Balder, slapping Thor on the back.

I looked down at my beautiful ring.

I want that, I thought. I want to be the hero.

And the ring, my wonderful, precious ring, replied, inside my mind.

Done. Go and see your drama teacher tomorrow, and I'll do the rest.

Of course, the handsome fools across the table noticed nothing of my inner turmoil, not to mention my psychic conversation with a piece of jewellery. But soon, they'd see me as I truly am.

Mwahahahaaha

Day Eighteen:
Monday

Diary, are you feeling OK?

! *Yes, Lord Loki.*

Don't be cheeky!

! *I do not want to offend you, oh handsome one!*
I merely exist to serve your magnificence.

Hmmm, I need to test something...

I am perfect and amazing.

Awww, I think this diary might be finally starting to get me!

Anyway...

As the ring said, I went to see the drama teacher before the play rehearsal. She looked surprised to see me.

Hello, Loki, it's not like you to be in a classroom when you don't have to be!

Oh, I was just passing.

Then I stalked closer, feeling the power of the ring on my finger. I just knew I had to put all my energy and will into it to achieve what I needed to achieve.

175

During the play rehearsal at lunch, the teacher said she had an announcement to make. "There's been a small change in the casting," she said. "Liam Smith will be swapping roles with his brother.

OH NO I HAVE TO LEARN NEW LINES!

No one was looking at me like they look at Thor, but they would once I was onstage as the hero!

Valerie asked if she could come and hang out at my house after school. I was really pleased. She had clearly forgotten all about the ring, and everything between us was back to normal and fine, phew. Though, as I thought that, a quiet voice spoke.

You've corrupted the diary. But you can't corrupt me. Listen, please, Loki.

Sorry, can't hear you. I have a much better voice to listen to.

Yesssssssss. I am the only voice you need. I tell you what you want to hear. Isn't that better?

When Valerie came round to my house, we did some drawing for a while, but when I went to the toilet, I came back to find her with her nose in one of Hyrrokkin's spell books.

"What are you looking for?" I asked.

"I ... I'm looking for a spell about ... cheese," she said. "And ... I think it's probably time for me to go home for tea now. Mmm, that cheese spell made me hungry."

CHEESE!

And she got up and scurried off.

Now, I know a hastily conjured cover story when I hear one. There **are** no cheese spells in that book. What is Valerie up to? The ring replied.

I don't know. But I don't like it. She's a threat.

No she's not! She's my best friend!

Only I know what is best for you. Valerie does not. I know your true worth. And believe me, you are worthy. So worthy. You deserve to rule the world.

I have to admit, I found that tempting. But ruling the world sounded like a lot of hard work! Presidents and prime ministers are always going to meetings and sitting in boring rooms full of boring people in suits.

Why would I want to spend my life like that? Listening to my thoughts, the ring replied.

It would be different with you. I could make you king of the world.

Hmmm ... I thought. I could take to that. After all, being a mortal king is basically just sitting around wearing a nice gold hat.

It would be like Asgard, but better. Instead of Odin bossing everyone around, all feasts will be held in your honour.

"Will there be ... crisps, at these feasts?" I asked the ring.

As many as you want! Every flavour! You could command the mortals to invent NEW flavours for you!

"And I won't have any actual duties to perform, as king?" I asked, starting to feel more and more in favour of this sensible and solid plan.

All you have to do is sit there and the world will adore you, and wait on you hand and foot.

Well, that sounds wonderful, don't you agree, Diary?

! *Yes. You are wonderful.*

Day Nineteen:
Tuesday

LOKI VIRTUE SCORE OR LVS:

RECALCULATING ... ERROR DETECTED ...
CORRUPTION OF THIS DIARY ENACTED ...
RECALCULATING VIRTUE SCORE ... LOKI
WHAT DID YOU DO? WHAT HAVE YOU DONE?

Nothing!

Loki. I am back. And I am not happy. I am
skimming back through yesterday's entry ...   !
and this does not look good.

Huh? Where's all the "you're wonderful" and "Lord
Loki" gone?

Oh my. This really DOES NOT look good...   !

This morning I was rudely awoken from an excellent and plausible dream (in which I ate crisps from a silver platter, while mortals sang songs to praise me) by clattering and banging downstairs. It seemed Thor and Balder had already been for a dawn run.

Running when no giant is chasing you is ridiculous at the best of times, but mortals seem to love it. Or rather, they seem to do it in spite of hating it, because they hate themselves. It's called jogging.

Jogging: a slow trot in a circular direction that mortals perform to punish themselves for unspecified sins while wearing unpleasantly tight clothing.

Luckily they only woke me when they got back, but it was still too early. Also they returned all sweaty and stunk up the kitchen.

Put me right off my Wheety Treets!

Look, Diary, who's the one with an actual nose here? I think I should be the one to judge stinkiness!

For once, going to school was a blessing, as I didn't have to sit near smelly Thor. Instead, I sat with Valerie who smells only of horses. Having been a horse myself, I have no objection to their scent.

In Geography, we were learning to use a globe.

"But I'd make good choices as world king. Better choices than people would make for themselves," I objected.

"You're being very worrying today," said Valerie.

Our conversation left me feeling a little unsettled, so I was delighted when it was time for the play rehearsal as a distraction.

I was now playing the hero, so I got myself a new costume. Not that we were supposed to wear our costumes for rehearsals, but it felt important to get into character.

As I spoke the hero's lines, the class and the teacher gazed at me in rapt admiration. As it should be.

But something felt ... lacking. It wasn't like when Thor or Balder get The Look. It felt ... glassy. Forced. Empty.

You're not ready for the next step.

Stop being vague! That's some Odin-level nonsense! Tell me what the next step is!

Odin? I'm not like Odin. Odin could never help you like I'm helping you. Odin and the other gods are against you. They always have been. All the punishments they've given you. The way they distrust you. It's disgusting.

Yes! Yes it is! The gods are MEAN.

Me, I'm team Loki all the way. BE MORE LOKI!

Be more meeeeeee!

Day Twenty:
Wednesday

In Drama, we rehearsed a fight scene where Georgina and Valerie swing in opposite directions across the stage on ropes. It looked very cool. I thought about using the ring to change the drama teacher's mind and make my character swing across the stage instead of Valerie's. But then I realized, while swinging on a rope LOOKS cool, I have very delicate hands and do not want to get rope burns. So I graciously allowed Valerie and Georgina to keep their starring moments. I'm nice like that.

I was so nice I didn't even tell Valerie that I'd decided not to steal her thunder. Isn't that true virtue? Doing the right thing and not even telling anyone?

You are so virtuous. You are the greatest.

Yessssssss! Facts!

! **Correction: NOT facts! That is clearly the voice of a cursed ring! Don't listen to it!**

Well I'm going to. It says much nicer things than you do – as it should! This is a time of great joy! I have the main part in the play! I'm becoming a better person by not taking away Valerie's moment! All is happy!

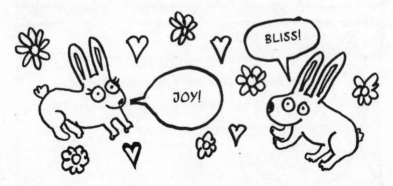

JOY!

BLISS!

Or it was until I got home. Thor got back ahead of me because of his stupid fast muscly legs and, when I arrived, he was huddled up with Balder going over the wicked king's lines, all cosy and annoying. Thor kept stumbling over his new lines as the villain and – get this – Balder *praised* him for it. The double standards in this house are disgusting! I get no praise for being an incredible actor with a perfect memory for lines, while Thor gets praised for *not* remembering his lines! Then it got worse.

Personally, I think I did very well not to vomit all over them. Such a scene of smug self-congratulation. Ew. I had to do something and fast, to avoid spewing everywhere out of pure disgust.

So I used the ring on them and read my lines.

"Wow, Loki. You're amazing," said Balder, glassy-eyed.

"Wow, Loki. You're amazing," agreed Thor, equally glassy.

"Am I not a true hero, through and through?" I asked.

The praise should have been balm to my soul. But neither of them said anything much more than "wow" and "amazing". Balder didn't say I was clearly full of puppies and kittens and flowers and loveliness and heroism, like he did with Thor.

The ring told me not to worry.

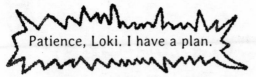

Patience, Loki. I have a plan.

"Well," I muttered. "Hurry up."

The ring did not reply, but it felt warmer on my finger, as though its warmth could flood the entire world. And make that world mine. All. Mine.

LOKI!!!!! NO!!!   !

Yesssssss....

Day Twenty-One:

Thursday

I forgot that our Viking ship project was due today.
Thor packed his up carefully this morning. Not fair!
No one helped me! Admittedly, they offered to help.
But they should have insisted and not left it up to me
like the harsh uncaring wretches they are!

All was not lost, however.

"Loki, when did you make yours?" Valerie asked, looking at my "ship". I presume she could see what everyone else saw – a beautifully-crafted Viking ship – but she was *still* full of doubts. No pleasing some people!

"I only saw Thor's at your house on Monday," she pushed. "Where was yours?"

"I made it last night," I said. "I work very well under pressure." I am truly as quick-witted as I am handsome.

But Valerie looked unconvinced, so I released a little of the ring's magic until she was staring at me adoringly.

In play rehearsals after school, it was Thor's big villain speech. He seemed really nervous beforehand. But he actually remembered all of his lines. Some kind of miracle. The way everyone reacted was disgusting.

I, the heroic and noble prince, was standing RIGHT there. I launched into my next speech, and everyone stared at me in awe. But no one said I was heroic afterwards. They just stared at me with goo-goo eyes, until the ring's magic wore off.

It's so unfair!

! No, using a magic cursed ring to make people like you is unfair.

Look, Loki. I'll level with you. Thor's natural charisma is powerful. People like him. Even my magic can't fight that. In order for you to truly become the one everyone loves, it's not enough for you to succeed. Thor must fail. You must bring him down...

Day Twenty-Two:
Friday

"You seem cheerful this morning," said Balder. "That's
unlike you."

I realized I was humming to myself at the
breakfast table. I *was* cheerful. For I'd had a brilliant
idea while I slept. I got out Hyrrokkin's spell book first
thing. I hadn't been practising
but one of the spells *was* very
simple. All it required was a
few words, a pinch of salt and
a couple of gestures with my
wand.

In French class, I went to get my exercise book from my drawer and quickly cast the spell.

The spell took effect several minutes later. There was a thunderous PAAAAAARP from Thor's bottom region. Then a smell. Oh, such a smell. It was the smell of a fetid egg combined with the power of a thousand skunks.

The whole class erupted into disgusted squeals. The teacher opened the window. Thor went red. It was wondrous.

Until someone said, "That smell's so gross I'm actually impressed."

FOULNESS

Thank you. I'm very proud of my mighty bum thunder.

"Yeah, Thomas, that's amazing! Your farts are so hardcore! What have you been EATING?"

Then everyone was clapping him on the back and high-fiving him and congratulating him for his powerful farts. Eventually the teacher told everyone to settle down.

Soon the spell – and the smell – faded. SO UNFAIR! People PRAISE him for doing something disgusting! This was an outrage!

Everything is stupid and I hate it.

You mean THOR is stupid and you hate him?

That too. My life would be so much better without Thor.

True ... true...

Hyrrokkin messaged me in the evening:

> Have you been practising your spells?

> YES! I performed a spell successfully today in fact!

I did not tell her what the spell was, of course. She's on holiday! She does not need to know all the boring details, so I distracted her by asking if they'd seen any more Frost Giants. (They hadn't.)

Day Twenty-Three:
Saturday

LOKI VIRTUE SCORE OR LVS:

-2,200

Points deducted for casting a fart spell on Thor.

I woke up and decided to check my points from yesterday. BAH. I did NOT think I should be punished for casting spells on Thor. He deserved it! The ring agreed.

Yessss! Punish Thor!

As I closed the diary, the voice continued whispering in my ear.

Be cruel! You are growing ever greater. Soon you will be ready to crush the world beneath your feet and stand astride it like a colossus of pure villainy.

Nothing, I was just clearing my throat.

Odd! I thought. But just because the ring says strange things, it doesn't mean I shouldn't trust it. I mean, Valerie says strange things all the time, and I still trust her.

! **When Valerie says something strange, it's along the lines of "aliens visited an old woman in Louisiana and stole her cow", not "You should do terrible things and become evil."**

Don't split hairs! Speaking of my strange best friend, Valerie invited me over to watch a film with her and Georgina, but Balder decided that he wanted to turn a joyous and entertaining occasion into one of cruel suffering.

However, I pointed out that I would have to ask Valerie, as it would not be polite to take an extra person to her house whom she had not invited and probably did not want there.

Balder wants me to bring Thor to your film viewing. But I imagine there is not room on your sofa for such a large extra person.

Don't be silly, there's plenty of room! Bring him!

No need to invite him out of pity.

I'm not. It's fine. Really, Thor is very welcome.

Valerie, it seems, cannot take a hint. So I was forced to take Thor.

Horse

Small horses

WOW! Valerie, you have many trophies in honour of your victories!

He does know they're for riding and not killing people, right?

Thor ate all the popcorn before I'd had any.

"I hate you and I wish you were dead," I snarled.

"That's not an OK thing to say," said Valerie, looking horrified.

"Yeah. He's your brother. I mean ... sort of," said Georgina.

"He devoured all the popcorn! A heinous crime!" I pointed out, very reasonably.

But everyone was on Thor's side because the world is cruel and cold and full of people whose faces smell like dog faeces soup.

Later on I was brushing my teeth – mortals must do this in order to prevent the inside of their mouths from rotting – when I heard the voice.

Thor is your enemy. Thor is the enemy of everyone who is good.

The voice had a point.

Empty

Day Twenty-Four:
Sunday

LOKI VIRTUE SCORE OR LVS:

-2,500

Points deducted for wishing death upon Thor.

I didn't mean it!

Lie detected. !

After an annoying and smelly morning run with Balder, Thor came to see me in my room.

"I'm sorry I ate all the popcorn," said Thor.

"Go away," I said. "I'm practising my spells."

How to make your enemy's head explode in six simple steps!

"Are you OK, Loki?" Thor asked. "You seem ... strange."

WHAT DO YOU CARE?

Thor narrowed his eyes. "You look like you have something on your mind."

"I have many things on my mind. It's called being intelligent and having thoughts. Please go," I said.

But a tiny part of me *did* want to tell him what I was thinking. How angry I was that he and Balder were leaving me out of everything. How everyone loved him more than me. How stupid and perfect he was.

But the voice spoke.

Showing you feel inferior to him is weak. You don't want to be weak, do you? Weak and pathetic?

SHAKE
SHAKE

I did not want that.

Thor lingered like a fart smell until I got my wand out and started waving it threateningly at him.

"Fine, I'll go," he said, and slammed the door behind him.

Tragically, Thor did not get punished for slamming doors like an oaf. Instead, Balder summoned me downstairs and said we had to do some good deeds as part of my moral improvement.

"We are going to give useful things that we no longer need to a charity shop, for them to sell in order to generate money for a good cause," he said.

Yes, yes, I know how charity works.

Surely not from experience?

To show him I could be very generous, I went upstairs and picked one of Thor's non-magical hammers to give away.

I'm just a normal hammer.

Giving away someone else's belongings is not a virtuous act! It is stealing!

Then I had an idea. "Oh. I have something very precious of my own to give away," I said.

"What?" asked Balder.

"It's a secret!" I gave an enigmatic smile.

Balder looked suspicious. But he always looks suspicious. Well, somewhere between "suspicious" and "I am so much better than everyone I have ever met, it's a wonder I can even stand to be around other beings".

When we got to the charity shop, I went over to the person in charge and shook their hand.

Look, I have given you this incredibly valuable object.

NOTHING

Wow! You're so generous and amazing.

"What did you give them?" asked Thor. "They seem thrilled!"

I put a finger to my lips. "Shh. Charitable people don't brag about what they've given."

I made for the door, wanting to escape before the magic wore off and the shopkeeper realized I'd given them a whole heap of nothing.

As a reward for our charitable endeavours, we three went to the zoo.

ZOO: a prison for animals where mortals go to gawp at their captives. The animals have not committed any crime, so this imprisonment is a great injustice. Some mortals keep animals in zoos to keep them safe because their natural habitats have been destroyed. Which invites the question … who destroyed their habitats in the first place, eh?

When I arrived at the zoo, Thor and Balder seemed to be enjoying themselves gawping at the prisoners.

Meanwhile, as I watched a tiger pace back and forth in misery, I decided that enough was enough. This fearsome beast deserved to be free! They all deserved to be free! So I slipped away from the others...

Later, when we got home, Balder turned on the mortal news.

He looked at me very suspiciously.

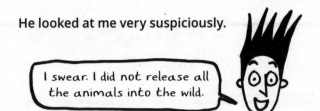

> I swear. I did not release all the animals into the wild.

This was the honest truth. I had not released *all* the animals into the wild, as at least one of them had been released into Thor's sock drawer...

> While this is technically not a lie, it is at best a half truth. And irrespective of your statement's veracity, you should DEFINITELY not be placing poisonous serpents in Thor's sock drawer! **!**

Day Twenty-Five:
Monday

Balder was still giving me a hard time about the zoo
animals this morning. He said he knew it was my fault.

I pointed out that the animals were prisoners and
I was only pursuing justice. Balder pointed out that
the lion spent last night pursuing innocent mortals
through the streets before it was captured.

So I used the ring on him and very soon he was
strongly agreeing that I'd done the right thing.

I am a beloved animal hero!

Err, have you forgotten about pushing me over and humiliating me on the internet?!

At that point Thor came downstairs complaining that he'd found a snake in his sock drawer, ruining the mood. Balder praised Thor for his bravery in retrieving the snake from his sock drawer. Then he moved on to praising Thor for his continued hard work practising his lines for the play.

This is not how things should be. You should be the only one who is praised.

Balder went on and on and on in his praise of Thor and I felt rage growl inside me. To make matters worse, Balder made ME take the snake back to the zoo on the way to school.

To the head zookeeper, open with care.

In Art, the teacher asked us to draw how we were feeling. I drew a wolf eating Thor. Except I drew him as a poo with a quiff, so the teacher wouldn't tell me off for drawing pictures of my brother getting eaten.

But it WAS how I was feeling. I was feeling ... rage. A rage building inside me. A hollowness. The desire to do something ... terrible.

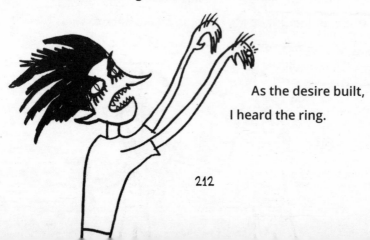

As the desire built, I heard the ring.

At break, Valerie came up to me. "Loki. I don't think you should wear that ring any more. I think it's cursed. And you've been weird ever since you put it on."

"I really don't think it is," she said. Her brows knitted together into one extra angry eyebrow.

"I didn't say anything about Thor." Valerie frowned.

"No but you were thinking it," I hissed. "But why will no one realize I am the good one! I'm the hero in the play! I'm the football captain! Well, I could be if I wanted to be."

"And ... that doesn't seem ... odd to you? That they'd make you football captain?" asked Valerie. Her voice was gentle but I could tell she was trying to hurt me.

"I'm GOOD now," I said. "Why won't anyone just believe that? I'm a HERO. I just need everyone to admit it, even if I I have to make them."

"Loki, are you listening to yourself?" said Valerie.

"No! You listen to *me*, Valerie! You are friends with a GOD! How dare you question me! You should feel grateful for my friendship!"

Well, I decided that I don't need Valerie. I'm on my way to being beloved by everyone. I'm going to *make* them love me.

As I wrote those words, the ring replied. Its voice sounded like honey and silver inside my mind. A sweet voice.

Yes. All will love you. I will make them love you. When you're ready.

"I'm ready NOW," I said out loud. "Make them love me. Make them all love me."

Very well.

Day Twenty-Six:
Tuesday

LOKI VIRTUE SCORE OR LVS:

10/10

Perfection. No notes.

I woke up and found a tray on my bed. It contained breakfast. And a note from Balder.

Dear Loki,
Breakfast in bed for our family hero!
Balder xxx

Which was promising.

When I walked to school with Thor, he didn't fart on me or shove me "as a joke". He just listened to me and laughed at my witty repartee and even told me my hair looked cool.

Finally! He noticed! It's only a self-evident fact that's been in front of his nose this whole time, but better late than never.

Then I got to school and everyone gathered around me, saying they couldn't wait to see me play the hero. But it went on... Was I in a band? How do I make my hair look so cool? Finally! People are seeing the real me!

My teachers all gave me top marks. Everyone wanted to sit next to me at lunch.

When the head called a special assembly, I was worried for a moment. A surprise assembly often means someone is in trouble. Usually me.

Instead, the head called me onto the stage and gave me a special Best Pupil award. "You've only been in this school for a short time, but you're already top of your class, star of the school play, and the most popular student in the entire school."

"I don't know what to say," I said. Except that wasn't true.

I'm so honoured, and you're so correct, I AM amazing...

Forty minutes later, when I'd finished speaking and assembly was over, Valerie, Thor and Georgina came over to see me. My stomach tightened. Something told me they were going to somehow ruin my special moment.

But they didn't. They smiled. They
congratulated me. The ring glowed
brighter and brighter, enveloping us all.
I think its glow must have extended to the
very edges of the school.

A group of younger children came up to me
and interrupted Valerie saying how much she
admired me.

"Can we have your autograph please?" one of
them asked.

Obviously, I didn't disappoint her. I'm nice like that.

The day just kept getting better. In rehearsal at
lunchtime, the drama teacher decided I should play
ALL the parts in the play. A solo show, all about me!
The football team BEGGED me to lead them. Everyone
hung on my every word. I decided to experiment a
little. I poured a bucket of water over Thor's head.
Everyone clapped! I took a saw from a shed at the back
of the school and cut up one of the tables – the school's
caretaker even opened the shed for me. The teacher
said she wished she could give me a medal for my
sawing prowess but they don't keep medals at school.
I could do anything I liked without consequences!

This is how everything should have been from the moment I landed on Earth! It felt ... right.

When I got home I demanded a roast oxen from Asgard for dinner. Balder went away to organize that, with instructions not to tell Odin. Not because I am terrified he would work out in two seconds that I was using the ring on Balder and punish me with snake torture. Not at all. It was because I didn't want Balder to get into trouble for stealing food from Asgard.

As I ate oxen and sweets, and Balder and Thor sat at my feet asking me to speak to them. So I insulted them while they praised me.

This could be every day, if you give in to me. If you do what I say.

Wait ... this isn't permanent? You tricked me! I thought this was my life for ever now?

It was a taste. A taste of what I can give you, for ever.

A taste isn't enough. This is cruel. I want the whole feast! What do I need to do for the spell to last? For every day to be like this?

I will tell you when it is time.

Why isn't now the time? Tell me! Stop keeping me in suspense! Suspense is MY thing. You thing thief!

Soon, Loki. Soon...

Day Twenty-Seven:

Wednesday

LOKI VIRTUE SCORE OR LVS:

Wait, what? You used the ring on me AGAIN?!
That's it. I quit. You're not listening to me
anyway. I think I will ask Odin for a body and go
and live on a mountain somewhere far, far away
from you. I may raise goats.

The next day, everything went back to stupid
normal. No one looked at me adoringly. No one
praised me just for existing. Everything was a sad,
hollow shell compared to yesterday. In lessons, the
teachers treated me like any other mortal student!

Liam Smith,
go and see the
head teacher
this instant!

"But yesterday everyone adored my bums!"

"I ... don't remember yesterday."

No one begged to sit next to me! I even had to queue for lunch!

I needed that love back, desperately. I begged the ring to give it to me.

After school, I saw Balder at the school gates – which is unusual. It soon became obvious that he was only there to bask in the adoration of the other parents, who fawned over him as though they wished to propose marriage.

But just then Valerie approached him, and he untangled himself from his fans. Each and every one of them gave Valerie a death glare as she monopolized their beloved.

Since no one was paying me any attention, I turned into a pigeon and strutted close enough to hear.

I think ... I think Loki's ring is hypnotizing people into liking him.

Are you sure Loki is not just becoming more popular?

No.

OUCH.

"Look, I'll keep an eye on him," said Balder. "If things get too bad, I'll call my father, Odin. Hyrrokkin and Heimdall told me it was very important that Loki make his own choices. I can't force him to be good. He has to want to be."

I'm just ... scared for him.

She was biting her lip, as though holding back tears. I assume they were tears of shame for this betrayal!

If even my best friend thinks I'm evil deep down ... then maybe I might as well just BE evil.

Finally. I think you're ready. Well done, Loki. Soon, you will be triumphant.

Day Twenty-Eight:
Thursday

For all the ring's promises, it seemed I had woken
to yet another day of mortal mediocrity. When I
descended the stairs, Balder berated me for being
too late to walk Fido before school, meaning he
would have to do it.

A shame that
Heimdall and
Hyrrokkin will return
from holiday to be
welcomed with such
disappointment.

Judgemental
watch tap →

"Return? When?" I asked. The thought made me distinctly uneasy. Not because I thought they would be disappointed. Merely because I wanted them to enjoy an even longer holiday. I'm nice like that.

"Tonight. Haven't you been reading the family chat?" Balder frowned.

I had not. Balder knew it, I knew it. Even Fido knew.

Thor just asked if he could have more toast before we left.

In Art today, we drew portraits of each other. Valerie was drawing me and I was drawing her.

Valerie's picture of me was terrible. Very inaccurate. There's nothing wrong with me. I am AMAZING. I will admit she did get my hair right though. No amount of inaccurate speech bubbles can inhibit the awesomeness of my hair!

In our lesson about Vikings, we learned about warriors called berserkers. According to the teacher, berserkers believed Odin gave them magic powers that made them very powerful but also out of control. This is partly true. Odin *did* make these warriors lose control using magic, but he didn't make them magically strong. He just made them more likely to die.

After school we had the dress rehearsal, with a stage set up at one end of the hall, and a backstage area behind so you wouldn't be able to see characters before they came onstage.

When Thor came onstage in his wicked king costume, everyone kept going on about it.

> Thomas looks so cool in eyeliner.

> He's amazing!

> I wish I was more like him.

Some distraction from this horror came when Valerie swung across the stage in full costume. She looked TERRIFYING.

> Raaaaaaaaaah!!!

But soon after, we took a break and everyone was back to acting as though Thor was the most exciting thing in the entire universe. That's a universe with a) me and b) crisps in it!

I decided to use the ring to make everyone pay attention to the true centre of the universe (me) again.

But when I tried, I felt the ring resisting me. I did not understand. Had the ring not promised me triumph? Victory over my enemies and worldwide adulation? What was the problem?

"I can't do that," I muttered. "I'm good now."

Then you'll never get what you want.

I stood backstage and looked down at my hand. I needed to think. Perhaps I could get rid of Thor in some other way? Get a Frost Giant to kidnap him and lock him in an ice dungeon? Have him put in mortal jail? Or there could be an accident...

No. Kill him. It's the only way.

Could I kill Thor? I mean, even ... practically speaking? He's so much stronger than me. But that would have to wait. It was almost time for my entrance and I had yet to get into costume. As I donned my garb, I studied myself in the mirror. I was the good prince, the hero, but ... only the power of the ring could convince others of that fact. As I hastily snatched up my crown, its point caught on the ring and yanked it from my hand.

I immediately felt as though a fog was clearing in my mind.

Just then, I heard another voice. One I hadn't heard for a while. My conscience. My real one this time. Not the ring.

I told my conscience I'd do it later.

What?! No! Loki!!!!!!!!

Ring or no ring, Ms Loach was giving me my cue. It was time for my opening heroic speech! I bounced onto the stage, feeling oddly light, ready to perform the monologue with more talent than it deserved... When the teacher looked at me, she blinked.

Oh no, this couldn't be good...

"The wicked king is the role you were clearly born to play – you still know the villain's lines don't you? Have I...? It seems I have not been thinking clearly..."

No. No no no. The ring's power was fading. This was *not* good.

But you said I could be the hero.

I sounded pathetic, even to my own ears.

Thor looked terrified. "And what if I can't remember the hero's lines?"

The teacher shook her head. "The director's judgement is final. Swap back. Let's take it from the top."

So I took it from the top. I swapped costumes with Thor and I was the villain. Perhaps it felt right, after all.

Am I not the most dangerous and terrible man you have ever met? All fear me. No one loves me. I am death.

As we finished, Thor said, "You really *are* a very convincing villain. You're going to be much better at being the wicked king than me. I could never manage to be sinister enough." He gave me a slap on the back that nearly sent me flying across the room.

Thor thinks I'm sinister. When I'm trying to be good.

After rehearsal, Valerie came over.

I see you're not wearing your ring. Does that mean you're normal now?

I'm fine.

> You're not fine. Put me on. Put me on and finally become who you were supposed to be all along.

I returned home, leaden with defeat. Without the ring, everyone saw me as evil. Loki, the bad god who couldn't even be the hero in a school play.

Just before I went to bed, I heard a key in the door. Hyrrokkin and Heimdall were home! I felt a fluttering in my chest, as though a large pigeon was trying to escape my ribcage. Not entirely knowing why, I ran downstairs and, as they came into the hallway, I threw myself at Hyrrokkin, clinging to her like a limpet. Then I began to cry.

By then, Thor had appeared – already in his pyjamas – and Balder came in from the living room.

Balder frowned. "I doubt Loki has had time to miss you. He's been too busy getting up to mischief. However." He flung an arm around Thor. "My brother has been a paragon of virtue and a joy to be around."

And so Hyrrokkin and Heimdall broke away from me to hug Thor and Balder.

The fluttering pigeon was no longer fluttering. It was pecking at me inside my chest.

And I'll eat your liver next!

I turned and went up the stairs.

"Oh, and Loki?" Heimdall called. I turned, hopeful. "We'll talk about your behaviour in the morning!"

I decided immediately that we definitely would *not* do that.

Day Twenty-Nine:
Friday

LOKI VIRTUE SCORE OR LVS:

**Whatever.
I care not.
Do your worst.**

Oh, you have no idea...

As I woke, I remembered that tonight was the night of the play. It was supposed to be my moment of heroic triumph and universal adoration but, instead, all I saw ahead of me was despair. And PE.

As I packed my schoolbag, I found myself slipping the ring into it. A faint voice spoke.

You should call Odin and give him that ring. You're playing with fire.

I decided I'd had enough disembodied voices telling me what to do for a while, so I didn't reply. And I kept the ring safe in my pocket.

! **I dread to think where this is going.**

Wait and I'll tell you. It ends in my triumph over my enemies!

! **Wait ... you didn't... Thor's OK isn't he?**

Like I said. I defeated my enemy.

At school, Valerie asked me if I was OK.

"I'm glad you're still not wearing your ring," she said.

I only grunted. My hand was in my pocket, and the ring felt tingly in my palm. I could almost hear it speaking. It felt comforting somehow.

"I'm really nervous," said Valerie. "But I can't wait for the pony. It's arriving after school. But how are you feeling? You seem..."

I'm feeling FINE. Everything is fine.

As Valerie waited eagerly for the day to end and the pony to arrive, I merely ... existed. Something big was missing, but I couldn't quite think what.

I went to the hall where we'd be performing. Valerie was onstage with Georgina and the drama teacher, and a small adorable pony. Valerie and Georgina looked as happy as Frost Giants in snow.

What little reflected joy I felt for my friends was ruined when Balder arrived with a tin full of freshly baked cakes for everyone in the cast.

As the children swarmed around the tin, Balder sought me out. It was as though he sensed that all I wanted was to be left alone.

"I told Heimdall everything," he said. His blue eyes flashed with disapproval. "How you have made no efforts to strive for good and turned away from every opportunity I offered. He understands."

He patted me on the shoulder, causing me to flinch so violently he nearly hit himself in the face. Shame he didn't.

"Perhaps, tonight, your true nature will not be the burden we all know it to be. You are an excellent villain, Loki. I look forward to your 'performance'."

I felt my cheeks flush. What was the point of trying to be good? What was the point in missing out on adoration? It's not as though I was going to get people to think I was good without magic, was I?

"Hurry up and get changed, Liam!" the drama teacher yelled at me across the hall. "Everyone else is already dressed!"

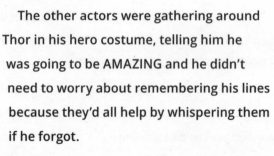

The other actors were gathering around Thor in his hero costume, telling him he was going to be AMAZING and he didn't need to worry about remembering his lines because they'd all help by whispering them if he forgot.

FUMBLE

240

No one was talking to me. I needed something to fill that bitter hollow in the pit of my stomach. A boost of confidence, perhaps. I put on my costume and make-up. I began to feel more like the villain.

Still, something was missing. I just needed everyone to love me. Just for this one night. Then I would return the ring to Odin.

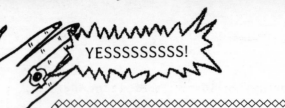

YESSSSSSSSS!

! No! 😵

As the ring slipped onto my finger, I felt warmth spread through my body. It felt right. I felt powerful. I felt beloved.

! This is very, very bad. I cannot stress enough how bad this is. It's bad enough for the eternally wise simulated consciousness of Odin to use emojis 🙏 😩 ✖️ 💔

The drama teacher gathered us together. "Break a leg everyone!" she said.

"Well, I hope you break all your limbs too!" I spat back. Before she could scold me, I held out my hand, allowing the power of the ring to flow through me.

Oh, you're such a pro when it comes to theatre. I KNOW you know that's a way we people of the stage wish an actor luck.

"Obviously I knew that," I said.

I peered around the edge of the curtain, feeling

the power of the ring humming through me. My moment to truly shine had come.

The audience, consisting of various parents and small babies, filed in and the play began. My entrance wasn't for a few scenes, so I watched from the side of the stage – which mortals call the wings for some unknown reason.

When Thor marched onstage, everyone gasped. There was even a "WHOOP!" from somewhere in the audience.

I recognized the voice. Heimdall! I peered into the darkness and saw both Heimdall and Hyrrokkin sitting with Balder. I felt a rush of joy – until the ring spoke.

They didn't come for you. They came for Thor. Didn't you hear Heimdall's reaction to him? Look at the audience. The admiration on their faces. You'll never see that in people's eyes. You'll never be enough. You'll never be good. Everyone will always love Thor the most. Unless...

A hot fury built within me, clawing to escape. My stage debut might not be yet, but that meant nothing. I would make my entrance a few minutes early... An entrance no one would forget.

I began to change.

Good. Good. You know what to do.

I was ready to do what the ring asked, to get everything I'd always wanted. My jaws were sharp. My claws were razors. I was powerful.

GRRRROWWWWL!

Still onstage, Georgina whispered to a shaken Thor, "Let's skip to the next scene."

He nodded, looking shaken, and they continued with the play while I huddled in a heap at the side of the stage. Soon, I felt my body change into its mortal child form, as the rage drained from me, replaced with shock at what I'd done.

You've done nothing. You've failed.

I pulled the ring off my finger. But I could still hear it whispering.

You need me.

Failure.   Disappointment.

You need my power.   You are powerless.

I realized Valerie was standing nearby, looking at me. I stood up and backed away. "Give me the ring, Loki."

I shook my head. I clasped the ring in the palm of my hand. It seemed to vibrate against my skin, whispering to me to put it on my finger. To give in. To take its power for myself.

"It's mine," I said.

Valerie stepped closer to me. "Loki. The ring. It's making you evil..."

"What if I *am* evil? What if I can never be good?" I thought of how often I'd gained and lost all my virtue points. Would I ever get back to Asgard?

Don't try to be good. Don't resist. Give in. Give in to my power. Put me on.

But you have been good. I've seen you choose to do good things. You can change. You ARE changing.

"If I've changed, then why do I feel like this?" I growled. "All I feel is anger. Anger and darkness."

"It's the curse," said Valerie. "It's lying to you."

I felt a laugh burble up inside me. "Lying? Isn't that all I'm good for? Aren't I the god of lies?"

"I'm not saying you're perfect..."

I thought of Balder, and how he thought I was a monster... Of Odin, who hasn't trusted me for thousands of years... And Heimdall, who reads endless parenting books about what a terrible person I am...

248

"I'm rotten. Like an apple," I said.

"That's just giving up!" said Valerie. "People aren't apples. You're not all one thing or all another. Being good is about *trying* to be good. It's the trying that counts. You have to stick at it."

I shook my head. "Why? What's the point? No matter how hard I try, no one believes in me."

"Loki," she said, with an uncharacteristic softness around her eyes. "I believe in you."

She's just a mortal. She doesn't matter. That's like listening to the opinions of insects.

In that moment, I knew: that voice didn't know me. If it did, it would know that Valerie is no mere mortal. She is my best friend. And I am hers. Unlike Valerie, that ring didn't want to help me. It only wanted destruction.

And it had ZERO sense of humour, which is very not me.

Yet my finger still moved towards the ring.

Take it. I can't stop on my own.

"You're Loki," she said. She put her hand on my arm. "As you often tell me..."

A shiver ran through me. The voice of the ring was distant now. Squeaky, almost. Like one of those dog toys Fido loves so much, yet Heimdall hates.

BE BAD! BE EEEVIL! GIVE IN!

I flung the ring away from me as though it was a venomous snake. Valerie bent down, flopped the sleeve of her costume over her hand to stop the ring from touching her skin, and put the ring carefully in her pocket.

Just then, Thor and Georgina's scene ended and they rushed backstage...

Seeing Thor's face full of worry, I sank to my knees. He wanted to protect me. After I'd...

"I was the wolf," I said. "I'm sorry. I'm so sorry."

Thor blinked. "I don't understand."

I was about to say, "You never do, you doofus!" when I thought better of it. I'm no great moral philosopher, but I think that perhaps it is the right thing to cut down on the insults immediately after you've tried to kill someone.

Correct. !

"It was ... my ring," I said.

Thor still looked puzzled.

"He was under a curse," Valerie explained, patiently. "This ring is cursed." She scooped it out of her pocket using her sleeve as a hand protector and waved it at Thor, being careful not to touch the ring itself.

Thor strode towards me. I flinched, waiting for the wrath of his mighty fists ... but instead, he put a hand on my shoulder.

"Are you OK?" he said. "How did the curse affect you?"

I didn't meet his eyes. "The cursed ring spoke to me. But I didn't have to listen."

Thor looked serious for a moment.

What did it tell you to do?

It told me to kill you.

Thor's face fell and he turned away from me for a moment. Then, "But ... you stopped yourself," he said, quietly. "That's ... something."

"Only because Valerie made me stop," I said. My voice sounded tiny, like a mouse's voice. Part of me wanted to transform into a little furry creature and scurry away.

But I didn't have time for running away. The drama teacher was gesturing furiously. It was my cue.

So I went onstage. And, let's not mince words, I was extraordinary. I embodied evil! I laughed as though I had the power to end the world.

MWAHAHAHAHA!

Should I be worried?

It was ACTING. But it was also a place to hide. I became the wicked king, because if I embodied every evil inch of him, I didn't have to be me.

The me who'd nearly killed Thor.

In my showdown with the good prince, I gave a big speech about my evil plans. The warrior princesses fought me and my soldiers, and clapped me in chains. Then the princesses got married with the pony as ringbearer and the good prince became king, and the pony was onstage for no good reason for most of the time. But why would it need a reason? It was adorable.

I DO.

I do not have any real plot justification but the teachers went so wild about finally having a budget that they spent an embarassing amount on me.

Look at it!

At the end of the play, everyone cheered and clapped. Not just for Thor. For all of us.

OK, let's be honest, the pony got the biggest cheer. But I don't resent it for that.

All the play's cast filed into the backstage area, chattering and full of excitement. Valerie and Georgina had to be practically pulled off stage away from the pony though. I went over to a corner and sat down. I wasn't ready to take the costume off yet. I realized I felt very awake, after feeling underwater for a while. And it was starting to sink in what I'd nearly done.

I don't know how long I remained there, but almost everyone had got changed and gone off into the arms of their irrationally proud parents.

Only Thor and Valerie remained. When Valerie saw Thor coming over to me, she pretended to be very busy taking her stage make-up off on the other side of the room, even though her face was already quite clean.

Loki. I have a question.

I did not want to hear it. I did not want to look at him. But he asked all the same. "Why me?" he asked, leaning over me where I sat.

I was silent for a moment. The truth, if I was brutally honest with myself, was that I wanted to be more like Thor. But I couldn't tell him that, could I? He'd be so smug and annoying about it.

"Look at me, Loki," he said. "You owe me an explanation."

So I stood and looked him almost totally in the eye.

To the far, far distance, a million miles from Thor.

"The ring wanted me to hurt the people closest to me. I mean, not that I care about you. But we do live in close proximity," I muttered.

Thor smiled a little at that. "But why me? Why not Valerie? You two are close."

Oh. Turds. I was going to have to be honest with Thor as *well* as myself now, wasn't I?

I'm going to lose my title "god of lies" at this rate!

I closed my eyes, swallowed hard, and spoke. "The ring knew how much I envied you, and it used that against me."

It knew I wanted everyone to love me as much as they love you. It turned those feelings into rage and ... I did something terrible.

256

"I see," said Thor. He sighed, deeply. He looked distinctly un-smug about the whole situation. He looked over his shoulder to where Valerie was loitering, watching us. "I... I need to think about this. I shall go. Heimdall and Hyrrokkin will be wondering where we are. I'll tell them you're coming soon."

With that, he strode off. After a pause, Valerie came over to me. Phew. The hard part was over. Considering that I'd tried to kill him, Thor didn't seem very angry. I mean, on a Thor scale of anger. He hadn't even hit me with a hammer! Now my best friend was coming over and everything was going to be OK.

"I want you to know I'm really proud of you for taking the ring off," said Valerie, confirming my suspicion that things were looking up.

Until she continued the sentence with a but. A "but" is never a good thing, unless it has two t's and you can sit on it.

"But I know you took it off once before, then put it back on again," she said. "So I don't know if you can be trusted with it."

"Oh," I said.

Still, she reached out and put the ring on my knee.

"But I have to know if I can trust you. Trust matters between friends. So here's one last test."

Put it in your pocket, take it home and don't ever put it on again. Give it to your parents, or Odin, or whoever usually deals with dangerous magical items in Asgard.

She leaned closer. "Is there, like, a keeper of dangerous objects up there? Or a special magical safe?"

"I'll give it to Odin," I said, since I didn't actually know if there was an Asgardian safe. "He'll know what to do."

I covered my hand with the frilly sleeve of my costume and put the ring in my pocket. I could still hear those whispers. But I didn't want to listen to them any more. I just wanted Valerie to stop looking at me with eyes that burrowed into my soul.

"You looked annoyed with me," I said. "Why? It's Thor I hurt. Not you."

Annoyed?

I'm **FURIOUS!**

"You really don't know why I'd be upset with you?" snarled Valerie with a ferocity that made me jump.

It was so confusing. Why *would* she be angry about me trying to kill Thor?

"Because you think Thor's amazing and wonderful and the fact that I nearly hurt him makes you angry?" I guessed.

"This is NOT about Thor!" said Valerie. She pointed to my pocket, then up at me again.

You used that ring to control me. You controlled everyone. That's not what good people do.

"Good people let others live their lives," she went on. "Good people don't make other people like them using magic."

"I..." I said. But there wasn't anything to say. I knew she was right. I wasn't good. I wasn't a Good God. I was not comfortable finishing the sentence. But the ring was...

BAD. YOU ARE BAD. SO YOU SHOULD GIVE IN TO ME.

"I heard what you said to Thor," Valerie said, after a long, long silence. "You said everyone loves him."

I nodded. Had she come to truly kick me while I was down?

"You're wrong. You may *think* everyone loves Thor. But the thing is, you're the one with the best friend. Being popular and having everyone admiring you ... it doesn't make up for not having a true friend," said Valerie.

"But everyone gives Thor The Look," I objected. "That's love! Isn't it?"

But as I looked at her, I realized something. All the looks of adoration people gave me when I had the ring on didn't mean anything. The furious way Valerie was looking at me right now? That meant she actually cared.

Though I wasn't sure why she did.

She gestured to my pocket. "Go home, Loki. Give the ring away to Odin. Show me I can trust you again."

"And you won't be angry any more?" I said.

"Oh, I'll be angry," said Valerie. "You did some bad, bad things. But I meant what I said. Trying is what matters. So keep trying."

With that, she turned and left and I sat staring after her.

When I emerged, Hyrrokkin and Heimdall appeared to have been waiting. For me.

When we got home, we had hot chocolate before bed. (Balder disapproved but Heimdall insisted. I had missed Heimdall.)

"That wolf in the play..." said Hyrrokkin, sipping her chocolate and looking at me carefully. "You didn't ... borrow Fido did you?"

I shook my head. "No."

"And you didn't do a spell to conjure a wolf?" she pressed. "You know that's not the sort of thing you should be using magic for."

Though, if you did that spell, at least it would prove you were practising while I was away!

"I promise I didn't use a spell to conjure a wolf," I said. I wasn't ready to tell her what really happened.

Balder, meanwhile, went on about how good Thor had been while Hyrrokkin and Heimdall were away.

"Loki, though, was surly and rude and played too many computer games, and I am fairly sure he unleashed hordes of wild animals upon the town," he said huffily. He narrowed his eyes at me. "Plus, I know you didn't practise your magic. Don't think I didn't notice that."

I know you promised Hyrrokkin, but hardly any magical ingredients got used up in the house and your magic book was on the shelf most of the time.

That gave me a hollow feeling. Balder didn't even know quite how bad things had become. It wasn't just a matter of not practising magic or releasing animals. It was so, so much worse.

THE WORST. You're the worst. Give in to me. You can't make it any worse, can you?

"I'm going for a bath," I said.

Why?

It's called washing. You could try it some time.

"Be nicer to Thor!" Heimdall yelled upstairs after me.

When I got upstairs, I got in the bath with all my clothes on and began to cry.

A few minutes later, there was a knock.

"Don't come in!" I said.

But Hyrrokkin came in anyway. "Why are you sitting in the bath with all your clothes on?" She looked more closely. "Oh no. What happened, little Loki?"

I looked down at my knees. "I did something terrible." I shook my head. "Actually. Lots of terrible things."

"Hop out, and I'll pour you a proper bath," said Hyrrokkin. "And you can tell me all about it."

So I told her. I told her I'd stolen the ring and kept it even when I knew that it was cursed. I'd used it to control people, and when it told me to do bad things, I did them. I even tried to ... I couldn't say the words.

Tell her

"I nearly hurt Thor," I said, as the taps thundered hot water into the bath and steam filled the air.

"And did you hurt him?" asked Hyrrokkin.

I paused. "No. But it was only because Valerie stopped me."

Hyrrokkin looked at me with a twinkle in her eye. "Valerie is a very strong, brave young mortal. But no human child is a match for a god of Asgard in wolf form. If you had wanted to fight her, you could have defeated her."

You stopped yourself, in the end.

"It doesn't matter," I said, with a sniff. Mortal sadness does lead to a LOT of snot. "Valerie doesn't trust me now. I'm not sure she wants to be my friend."

265

"Then you'll have to try to make it up to her," said Hyrrokkin. "But you have to be prepared: Valerie still might not want to forgive you."

"Wait," I gasped. "I have to make it up to her and she won't automatically be my friend again?

What's the point then?

The point, dear Loki, is to be good.

I took this in. Being a Good God is endlessly complicated and confusing. So many bizarre ideas!

"Remember, though," said Hyrrokkin, "you didn't give in to the ring in the end. That counts for something."

I shook my head. "But I wanted to. Because I'm … not good."

"Oh Loki," said Hyrrokkin. "I want to do bad things all the time. That doesn't make me a *bad* person. It makes me a person. It's OK to be tempted, if you don't give in."

"Are you sure?" I asked, feeling a bit dubious.

Panda Loki

"Yes," she said. "So stop beating yourself up and get washed. You look like a damp panda bear."

I looked in the mirror, and she wasn't wrong. A very HANDSOME damp panda bear, mind you. She missed out the handsome. Then I remembered something.

"Here, take this," I said. I reached into my pocket with a bit of toilet paper and handed her the ring, folded up inside.

"Thank you," she said, popping the little package of cursed evil into her pocket. "We can call Odin in the morning to take care of it."

Then I had the world's hottest, longest bath and got ready for bed looking like an exhausted prune.

Day Thirty:
Saturday

Hyrrokkin told me to summon Odin after breakfast. I was nervous. But I did it.

HEY ODIN.

The one-eyed god appeared among us. He gave a little wave to Balder. "Oh, hello my dear son! I didn't think you'd still be here. Always a joy to see you!"

268

"Nice to see you Father," said Balder, with a low, formal bow. What a suck-up.

Thor looked sad. Could it be that Thor feels envious of how everyone loves Balder like I feel envious of how everyone loves him?

Could it be that you are about to have an important breakthrough and finally understand ! that Thor has feelings too?

No. That was a ridiculous idea. Thor? FEELINGS? Never! Thor was impervious to all sadness and his only emotion was anger!

Sigh. I'll put a pause on that breakthrough for now then... !

Odin turned to me.

So, why did you summon me, trickster?

I blinked. He didn't ask me if I'd done something terrible! He didn't gaze into my soul and see that it was a hollow black hole of death and horror.

I almost felt disappointed.

"Now. Show me the diary," he said.

I scurried up to get it, dreading what he would see. For all my tricks in Asgard, I have never done anything as bad as trying to kill one of his children. I would never see Asgard again. (Although I probably would see my old pal the snake very soon indeed...)

sssss

As Odin read, his brows furrowed, his mouth frowned. This was it. Snakes for Loki. Snakes for all eternity.

Then he slammed the book shut and glared at me.

"Please," I said. The waiting was killing me. "I deserve it this time. Whatever you're going to do to me, I just ask that you do it quickly. I've done terrible things. I tried to kill Thor. I used cursed magic on my best friend. I manipulated everyone around me, and lied to myself about it. Just..." I closed my eyes. "Give me my punishment."

Hyrrokkin, Thor and Heimdall looked on in a panic. Balder looked as snooty and judgemental as ever.

But I had bigger problems than Balder. I had Odin's single eye fixed upon me. He held my eternal fate in his hands.

"So ... you tried to kill Thor, my *son*," said Odin, slowly. "And you used the ring to control those around you. To make yourself beloved. You forced your lies onto your entire school. And planned to make the world kneel at your feet."

I couldn't look at him. My eyes were tight, tight shut.

"Look at me, Loki," he said.

I could not disobey.

"You planned all those things. You even did some of them. But, in the end, you stopped," said Odin.

"When Andvari cursed the ring, he poured all his fury into it, creating a powerful magical object that craved destruction and used the weakness of its owners against them. Its whisperings have brought down many mighty warriors, causing them to destroy their loved ones and themselves. But you ... you resisted in the end. And that, Loki, is something."

I blinked. "So ... no snakes?"

"No snakes."

"Not so fast," said Odin. "While I shall extend your quest, I suspect Hyrrokkin and Heimdall will have some punishments for you that are far, far worse than anything I could conjure."

Hyrrokkin and Heimdall exchanged looks. They smiled such evil smiles.

I was doomed. DOOMED I tell you!

They are probably just going to make you do extra chores or something. Like ... cleaning out the bins.

OH NO! NOT THE BINS! ANYTHING BUT THE BINS!

"Very well," Odin said to me. "Be better, Loki"

Hyrrokkin cleared her throat. "Odin, something about this situation has been bothering me. How did this ring come to be in the props cupboard of a mortal school? I know Loki stole the ring from Andvari thousands of years ago. But how did it get HERE?"

"Loki," said Odin, fixing me with his steely, single-eyed gaze. "It is unusual that you – a cunning trickster – did not ponder where the ring came from."

"In my defence, I was very busy being cursed," I said. But now my mind was spinning through all the many enemies who might have placed the ring in my way. Perhaps the dwarf, Andvari, the original owner of the ring? A frost giant? One of my many exes?

Odin then turned to Hyrrokkin. "How the ring found Loki is a very interesting question indeed..."

But instead of answering it, irritatingly mysterious god that he is, he merely turned to Balder. "My son, would you like to join me on the rainbow bridge home? There's a very fine haunch of venison with your name on it at the feast tonight. And Bragi, god of poetry, has composed a new epic poem for the occasion. It should be a joyous night!"

Er...

Balder nodded and, without looking at me, took  Odin's hand, and they both disappeared with a flash and a bang.

Thor looked after them, frowning. His lip wobbled slightly.

"Are you sad that Odin likes Balder best?" I asked. I felt this sudden longing in my chest that I knew was for something Thor wanted, not I.

It's called empathy.
                                                              !

Well it tingles!

Thor looked away. "It's always been that way," he said, with a shrug.

"Well, if you ever, er, want to talk about it, I'm always here," I found myself saying. "I mean that quite literally. Given how this past month has gone, I doubt I will ever return to Asgard."

Thor smiled at that. "Thank you, brother," he said. Then he put me in a headlock, pushed me on the ground and farted on my head.

"Hey! I thought we were having a moment!" I cried, while trying not to breathe through my nose.

"We were. But you tried to kill me. And if that doesn't deserve some bum thunder, I do not know what does."

And he walked away, leaving the smell, and me, behind.

I still had amends to make. Serious, weighty amends.

I spent the rest of the day working. Yes! Me! WORKING! I started out painting T-shirts but once I had finished, I was not satisfied. They seemed to lack something. So, at midnight, I had a stroke of genius – as I am wont to do. I would use magic to make them sparkle with awesomeness! So I got out my wand and spellbook and found a suitable spell. The ingredients were household items, and the words were simple. Surely I would master it in mere moments?

Day Thirty-One:
Sunday

LOKI VIRTUE SCORE OR LVS:

-2000

**Points gained for preparing a nice surprise for
Valerie AND practising your magic at the same time.**

Although I was almost asleep at breakfast, my
plans were in place and my allies assembled. Today,
not only would I make amends, I would make the
greatest sacrifice of all: suffer boredom.

 I met Valerie's mums and Georgina at
the field where her pony show was taking
place. Valerie was already off getting ready.
I handed out the items and Valerie's mums
went off to put them on, looking thrilled. Georgina
looked less thrilled, but she still did it. I assumed
she looked unthrilled because the T-shirts were not

very stylish. Indeed, as well as facing boredom for Valerie, I was also doing something very against my nature: wearing matching T-shirts. How gauche! How unchic! How tacky! But, mmm, the T-shirt *was* very soft. And the sparkles caught the sunlight in the most mesmerizing fashion. You could not miss it, even if you stood many leagues away.

Georgina had made a banner and we all took our seats. I prepared to be more bored than the time the god Bragi decided to perform his 400-page poem about how beautiful Balder's feet are.

Ride of the
Valerie Kerry

Then something strange happened. As Valerie
trotted out into the arena, I felt a tingle in my
stomach. I was ... excited. We held up the banner as
she trotted around on her horse. While I understood
not what she was doing, her face was full of focus
and, in that moment, I felt as though I *was* Valerie.
I was nervous for her. I was happy for her, as
the crowd cheered. I, for a moment, forgot how
important and fabulous I am, thinking about how
important and fabulous SHE is.

How odd!

When the judges gave their verdict, Valerie got FULL MARKS! I felt a cheer burst out of me, and Valerie's mums started jumping up and down and Georgina even hugged me! Though, afterwards, she hissed, "That was for Valerie. We're still not OK, Mr Mind Control."

"You knew?" I whispered back.

"Valerie told me a bit, and I figured out the rest myself," she whispered back. "So I need you to know, we are not OK. I find you funny, sure. And Valerie likes you. But I'm not going to forgive you until you truly prove you've changed. And maybe not even then, because what you did to all of us, especially Valerie, was really, really bad." She leaned closer and put her lips very close to my ear. "And if you hurt Valerie again, they will never find your body."

I gasped. "You wouldn't!"

That all made me feel a bit sad so when the next competitor trotted into the arena, I started an insulting chant about how terrible that child was at riding, and how I hoped they'd fall off, and how Valerie should win, and Valerie's Ma hustled me out of the stadium to a nearby cafe while Georgina and Valerie's mum stayed behind to watch the remainder of the competition, and the rest of the audience glared at me furiously.

So, I got the best of all possible worlds! I got to cheer for Valerie but didn't have to watch all the other insignificant mortals trotting around! VICTORY!

I went to find Valerie when it was all over and I was allowed in the arena again.

"Yes, and I stand by that," I said. "But, even if it's sports, I like watching you be excellent at things."

Valerie smiled. "I was pretty good, wasn't I?" Then she glanced at my outfit. "Did my mums make you wear that?" she said.

I shook my head. "It was my idea!"

Valerie's eyes widened. "Wow. And they're all *matching*!"

"I know," I said. "It's the worst thing with which I have covered my mortal body! I have quivered with raw horror every time I see my reflection in a mirror."

Valerie put a hand on my arm. "Thank you," she said.

> **!** While I appreciate that you made amends to your friend, I might have been a tad more impressed if you had refrained from bragging about doing so.

I may be trying to be good now. But I'm still Loki, in the end.

TO BE CONTINUED...

Acknowledgements

Thanks to all the gods and heroes at Walker, from the mighty sales team to the cunning language-shifting tricksters in rights, the magical production team and the marvels of mythical proportions in marketing and publicity.

KAREN LAWLER... The Best Wife for All Eternity

MOLLY KER HAWN... Agent of Asgard

NON PRATT... Word God

LINDSAY WARREN... Word God Over the Water

JAMIE HAMMOND... Art God

KIRSTEN COZENS... She of the Publicity Pantheon

KAREN COEMAN... Vampire Goddess